Mike Barnes

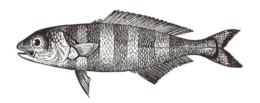

to andrew —

mike Barnes

The Porcupine's Quill

CANADIAN CATALOGUING IN PUBLICATION DATA

Barnes, Mike, 1955–
Aquarium

ISBN 0-88984-209-4

1. Title.

PS8553.A7633A88 1999   C813'.54   C99-931917-5
PR9199.3.B37A88 1999

Published by The Porcupine's Quill,
68 Main Street, Erin, Ontario NOB 1TO.
Readied for the press by John Metcalf; copy edited by Doris Cowan.
Typeset in Galliard, printed on Zephyr Antique laid,
and bound at The Porcupine's Quill Inc.

Represented in Canada by the Literary Press Group.
Trade orders are available from General Distribution Services.

We acknowledge the support of the Ontario Arts Council,
and the Canada Council for the Arts for our publishing program.
The financial support of the Government of Canada
through the Book Publishing Industry Development Program
is also gratefully acknowledged.

1 2 3 4 • 01 00 99

Canadä

to my family

Bill Mary Sue Chris Greg Sarah

* * *

Many people helped to bring this book to life, but I am particularly grateful to two men: Timothy Findley, through the Humber School of Writers, for practical advice on writing fiction; and John Metcalf, for timely boosts of confidence and belief.

Contents

The Aquarium

KEN SAW SOMEONE NEW at the April meeting of F.R.E.E., the lupus support group he occasionally attended. After the talk on 'Acceptance vs. Resignation', there was a refreshment break before the group discussions. He was reading the labels on an array of specialized crackers – Salt Free, Gluten Free, No Salt No Gluten – when he looked up to see a woman watching him from the other side of the room. She leaned forward on two metal canes, as on a balcony railing. He saw, besides the aluminum canes, shaggy blond hair, a bulky figure under a thick sweater, and a plain, kind face. A roomy face, as if the features had been pulled wide by a generous sculptor.

He turned away to hide the butterfly rash on his own face. The wing-like blotches came and went, but they were flaring that day. When he turned back she had joined a group at one of the tables. He was hailed by a group needing to be fleshed out, and was soon being pressed for his opinion on 'Anger: Friend or Foe?'

Two weeks later he saw her again. She was in the new pet store on Muskoka Road where he had gone to purchase an aquarium. A plump dark-haired girl of seven or eight was with her. As Mr Hecht, the owner, explained to Ken the start-up procedures for a 'freshwater habitat', the girl led her mother around to inspect the animals. They visited the fish, the birds, the reptiles and amphibians, and the mammals. They appeared to be regular customers, pointing and commenting on the welfare of old friends.

Ken noticed again the woman's frank, almost cavalier, way with her canes. She gestured with them, tapping on cages. His own cane remained in the closet except for the worst days, when he tried to stay indoors. She did not look at him, but he sensed somehow that she remembered him. It was a contraction in her roomy manner, as if curtains had been drawn against a draft. She seemed too interested in the baby mice.

At the cash register they drew up behind him. Mr Hecht nodded

9

at the small box in the girl's hand and asked Ken, 'Do you mind?'

'No. Go ahead.'

The woman smiled.

As they were going out the door, Mr Hecht called, 'Just once a day, Miriam. Remember what I told you. They always look hungry.'

Miriam, Ken thought, the daughter.

The set-up, as Mr Hecht promised, was not difficult. The diagrams in the various brochures helped to clarify the overly elaborate instructions. It was a disappointment to see how much of the equipment was made of plastic; Ken had expected thick glass and metal.

He washed the ten-gallon tank and upended it in the bathtub to drain. Then he rinsed his gravel. Mr Hecht had congratulated him on his choice of black and white. Most people were lured by the fancier colours, but fish showed up much better against a plain background. He took his time. Cold running water always soothed his knuckles, and it was an added pleasure to sift the small smooth stones, burrowing against the mild resistance.

He attached the air filters, one on either side, and the tubing leading through the top to the pump. As he scraped the plastic parts with a penknife to make them fit, his knuckles began to burn again.

He removed the canopy and filled the tank with buckets of tap water as high as the filter vents. He plugged in the pump to test it. Bubbles rose through the tube to froth at the surface. The gravel settled to the bottom by the handful. He mixed the black and white in pleasing patterns, his arms cool to the elbow.

It was working.

The rectangle of clear water was soothing, with its soft burping bubbles and humming pump. He still needed to get a thermometer and heater. The most vivid fish were from the tropics; room temperature was frigid to them. Plants (artificial were safest) and other decorations were optional. It took two weeks to establish the bacterial cycle, Mr Hecht said. Ken didn't see how a bacterial cycle could be established with simple tap water, but he supposed he would find out.

He lay down on the futon to rest. It had taken less than an hour. Still, his knees and hands, and his lower back, throbbed. Any bending or lifting – any *use*, damn it – did it. Yet it was supposed to be vital to remain active: don't lock up! The current compromise strategy was to follow activity closely with a rest period, preferably with his feet up. Increase circulation, then let it subside, reverse itself.

From the futon he looked up through clear bubbling water, topped and fringed by Sondra's herbs, at cloud-spotted blue sky. It made a beautiful picture. Like looking up from the bottom of a lake. The basil, parsley and thyme were lush. *Throw it out if you want,* Sondra had written from her new address. Offended by her nonchalance, Ken kept the herb garden flourishing. Soon after the note, he had turned on the TV and seen her pitching an antacid, dipping a naked rose, then a coated one, into a vat of hydrochloric acid, and frowning then grinning at the results. The absurdity of it had not quite modulated his envy that she had landed, so quickly, a paying job.

'Research your character,' she used to urge, when they were working together in a Pied Players production. She believed in exploring a part from all angles, through poetry, diary, dialogues, stories … 'whatever connects'. But, to Ken, research seemed a bit thick for amateur theatre. And anyway, he got as many laughs, and even a few tears, with his collection of tics and mannerisms. An unusual hat often worked wonders. 'Too technical,' Sondra warned gently. It wasn't just about applause.

After a while the humming of the pump became annoying. Vibrations shook it over the top of the bookcase until it rattled against the tank. He immobilized it with tape, over a cotton batting pad, which quieted it considerably; but now he wondered how loud it would seem at night. It might be necessary to move back into the bedroom, which for some time now had been made up and empty, like a guest room. Evening naps on the futon that segued into longer sleeps had started the habit. And it made sense to minimize movement. Even his doctor agreed that, all things considered, that was a good idea.

The name of the pet store was Fins, Tails & Feathers. But Ken remembered it as Scales & Feathers, then, recalling a third element, as Scales, Fur & Feathers. At this point a snippy operator cut him off, saying he should get a phone book. Watching the bubbles, he wished that Mr Hecht had chosen a less cute name. Pets, or the Pet Store.

The pump whined.

That afternoon, he went into Words to see if he could find a book on aquarium fish. Miriam's mother was behind the cash, leaning against the counter.

'Family planning?' she asked, when he had found his book and taken it to the front.

He smiled. 'It does feel a bit like that.'

She said, 'I think it's the best part of the whole process. Like choosing baby names. Before you get to the diapers.'

'I guess so,' he said.

As she rang in the sale, he noticed that the hand she left on the counter was white with the weight it had to bear. Her pale blue eyes were set in webs of fine lines that he understood: he had caught himself frowning, in mirrors and windows.

'What's the name of the pet store anyway?' he asked.

When she told him, he related the episode with directory assistance, dressing up the operator's surliness and his own helplessness for the sake of the story. Her chuckle – low, unforced – had the resonance of applause.

'By the way, I'm Ken Staines,' he said, before leaving.

'I know. I saw you in *Who's Got the Key?* You were good.'

'Thanks. What's your....?'

'Marie.'

'How do you ..?' he began, then changed the question. 'When did you start working here?'

Marie answered, 'Just a week ago. Mr Goshe hired me on the spot.' She nodded at the canes, leaning against the cabinet beside her. 'I guess a woman waving two of those is hard to refuse.'

Smiling back at her, Ken saw the space in her large features modulate to something more like preparation. Not an empty room, her face, but a comfortably furnished one.

They talked for a while longer, until Mr Goshe came to close up. At Marie's suggestion, they continued their conversation over coffee in Rombo's Café. More talk of aquariums led to a dinner invitation. Miriam would enjoy showing off her fish and how her tank worked.

'You don't look like you'll eat us out of house and home,' Marie said, with a frank look up and down him, as she reached for her canes.

* * *

Ken drove to the address she had given him. On the door of number 2 were several crayon drawings of fish. Looking at the coloured shapes, he hesitated a moment before knocking.

Marie introduced him as an actor.

'I remember,' Miriam said, her smile more vacant than shy, without taking her eyes off the dinner she was stirring in an electric frying pan.

It tickled but also unsettled Ken to have his hobby elevated into a career. 'The rent,' Marie said when he described his former job as groundskeeper at Birchwood. She smiled ruefully at his story of the generous severance cheque the lodge had given him, in gratitude, he suspected, for having the foresight to resign. But her frown at his phrase 'crippled gardener' told him he had taken the performance, as Sondra said, over the top. Milked it one drop too far.

Miriam made dinner. Between thorough-going stirs of the chili pot, she shredded lettuce and diced a tomato. She gave her full attention to these tasks, unfazed by his presence at the kitchen table. At the other end of the table, Marie sipped a Coke, either exhausted or trying to undo any impression of eagerness she might have given. Waving a hand at the fridge, she told him to help himself to pop or juice.

After a while she excused herself and came back dressed in a brown sweatsuit. Ken looked up to see her rushing at him – wobbly but headlong – then realized that she was not using her canes. They leaned against the fridge. She plopped down again in her chair, summoning a wan smile when he started another story.

After dinner they went into the living room to look at Miriam's aquarium.

Ken and Marie sat on the couch while Miriam tended to her fish. She suctioned out some dirty water by holding a plastic nozzle over the gravel bed and sucking on the end of a tube to start a siphon action, then letting it drain into a bucket. Ken moved forward to help but Marie held up a hand to stop him. Miriam added fresh water, measured in Stress-Coat, shook in food flakes. These actions, as grave and slow as her dinner preparations, had the look of memorized ritual. She opened a pet diary and, peering seriously into the tank, made notations in it.

Now Marie nudged Ken to go over to her.

Miriam barely glanced at him as he knelt beside her. Looking into her notebook, he was saddened to see that she was merely placing checkmarks beside a series of names – to indicate continued life, presumably. The names were not *names*, but species: leopard danio, black moor, fantail, gourami, bleeding heart tetra. Miriam stared intently into the tank. The water was still murky, with settling debris, as well as algae buildups in the corners and on the sides. A hollow, lime-green skull was filmed with slime. The fish, with one or two exceptions, were pale and thin, their fins ragged. Was that I C K? Dust on the canopy completed the impression that the project was beyond Miriam.

When Miriam disappeared down the hall, he prepared some questions about the aquarium, hoping to draw her out a little. After a while he asked Marie where she had gone.

'To bed,' Marie answered, stifling a yawn herself.

He left soon afterwards.

At home, the humming and bubbling sounded vaguely ominous, especially in the dark. The clear rectangle looked like a front now. Behind it lurked the slimy buildups and waning lives it was supposed to nourish. Already the water looked slightly grey.

A light. He needed a light.

At Fins, Tails & Feathers, Ken walked about with new eyes. The dingy, crowded cages and tanks seemed less depressing when you intended to buy an animal. You bonded, as Sondra would say, in the act of liberation. Miriam's tank, though dirtier than the store's, was at least a *personal* captivity. In some way, that mattered.

After studying the fish, he spotted a little translucent shrimp scavenging along the bottom of one tank. Ghost Shrimp, read the label. They had to be hardy. And useful, picking pieces out of the gravel.

'Don't rush things,' said Mr Hecht, chasing the agile shrimp with a small net. Ken said it was for a friend.

He drove around until he thought they would be finished dinner, stopping for a few minutes by the docks. The days were getting longer. The planks shone from the afternoon rain. He removed the plastic bag from its newspaper wrapping and held it up to the setting sun. Orange rays lit the water as the shrimp swam about. Wherever this cool globe travelled was its home. See-through flesh surrounded a thin dark core. Back legs churned like a tiny electric brush, while prehensile front legs explored the plastic. Long antennae drooped like the ends of a tightrope-walker's balancing bar. Did people eat the freshwater variety?

'Miriam, meet Jumbo,' he said, and watched her fingers tremble slightly as she opened the canopy to suspend the bag in the water.

Marie, on the couch, smiled. 'What do you say, Miriam?'

'Thank you.' Her eyes stayed on the shrimp in the bag.

When they released it, Ken holding the bag while Miriam cut the top with scissors and netted its captive – more expertly than Mr Hecht, with a sudden flip of her small wrist – the shrimp did a series of comical stunts: a handstand with its tail in the air on the plant, a slow somersault, a churning climb followed by an exhausted sink, before backing under the base of the No Fishing sign. Home.

'Jumbo,' Miriam said.

'Where did you get that name?' Marie asked.

'Well, it's better than Breaded. Or Fried.' Marie shook her head. Miriam, for the first time, laughed, a disconcertingly intense giggle.

'What's his name?' she asked, pointing at a fish hovering inside the skull.

Ken shrugged at Marie. 'Yorick?'

Marie groaned, and Miriam giggled piercingly again. It became a game. Miriam pointing at each fish and Ken, like Adam, naming them. A slow, wobbly swimmer was Lightning. The black moor was Othello. The bleeding heart tetra was Romeo, or Juliet – did they know? The glass tetra, Casper. They seemed delighted by his offhand invention. He felt vestiges of a magical power, of freewheeling caprice.

But when Miriam opened her pet diary, he saw that she wrote down 'Ghost Shrimp' and placed the first check mark beside it. The names were just funny sounds.

She turned off the light and stood up to go to bed; solemn-faced, her hands clasped at her waist.

'Thank you,' she said again.

'You're welcome, Miriam.'

He sat on the couch. Marie moved close and kissed him on the cheek. 'She's thrilled,' she murmured. Sensing a disproportion, he merely smiled. Marie put her head on his shoulder.

After a few minutes, she said, patting his hand, 'Why don't you tuck her in?'

Doesn't *she* have a say? he thought, but he went down the hall.

He was surprised, for some reason, to find Miriam propped up in bed with the light on, reading *The Lion, the Witch and the Wardrobe*. Her brow was furrowed in concentration.

'Good book?' he asked, from the doorway.

'Mm-hm,' she answered, her eyes on the page.

He remembered reading the story, remembered the time in his life when he had read it. A dark secret closet, stuffy with clothes, opening onto another world. An ice witch. A friendly lion. English children who missed tea time.

'Hard to read?'

'No.'

On the floor beside the bed were several notebooks. *Miriam Evers* was printed on the top one, under a pen and pencil and eraser.

'Good night,' he said.

'Good night.'

Ken and Marie were kissing deeply while Seinfeld and his friends joked about modern life. Her mouth tasted sweet and her lips were soft, almost too yielding. He found himself kissing her harder than he meant to.

'Can I turn that off?' he asked.

'Please,' she whispered.

They kept kissing, their kisses growing longer and less passionate, until Marie took his hand and raised herself off the couch. 'Come.'

In the room next to Miriam's it was pitch black. They undressed in the dark and got under the covers. Though they took it slow, the creaking and popping of their joints made a sound of radical intimacy, bones grinding upon bones. Marie came with a harsh squawk, which sounded even more forceful because Ken knew she was trying to restrain herself. His own orgasm travelled up his throat like a bubble, a clear wobbling globe, and escaped in a hiss.

Afterwards, Marie sniffled briefly, then became lighthearted. Her hands went to the tufts of hair on his head, tugging them gently and smoothing them over his bald spots. Bozo the Clown? Or was she trying to simulate another, remembered head?

Then she turned away on her side and, from behind her, he explored her body. This was new, to recognize more than marvel. Already he felt the contradictory tugs of an empathy that could deepen but also diminish passion. She had been sick longer than he had. Her skin hung loosely from her bones. Exercise was an insoluble problem: how to get enough without causing more damage.

They dozed. And then she said, 'We haven't talked about it at all, you know.'

'I know.'

'I'm glad.'

'So am I.'

'Do you think we can keep it up?'

'I doubt it.'

Her chuckle was bitter, or tentative. 'Just tell me one thing.'

'Sure.'

'How many doctors did you go through to get a diagnosis?'

'Five, I think.'

'And how long?'

'A few years.'

'Hmf. Assholes.' After a silence, she swung back to him and they had a giggling session, calling each other names.

'Hypochondriac!'

'Neurotic!'

'Complainer!'

'PMS!'

'C-F-S!'

'I like you.'

'I like you, too.'

She felt his forehead and cheeks. 'I guess this is a remission.'

'Yeah. I feel pretty good, lately.'

'Good. But that's enough, okay?'

'Agreed.'

Marie, warm as a half-filled hot-water bottle, nuzzled against his side. 'You made Miriam happy,' she said.

Not wanting to encourage more gratitude, he said nothing.

'I didn't tell you, but … she's in the Special Needs class at school. They've identified her.'

'Why?' The question slipped out with a hot anger.

Marie clutched his neck. 'Oh, thank you!'

He thought he understood.

Her digital clock said 2:00 when he woke up again. Marie was on her stomach, asleep. He shook her gently to tell her he was leaving.

'Why?' she murmured.

He couldn't explain that. Suddenly, it was very important to get home. He saw the sheen of her eyeball trained on the pillow case.

'Call me,' she mumbled, rolling over. But he knew her sleepiness was feigned, now. She was staring at the wall.

He was fitting the light into the aquarium canopy the next morning when the phone rang.

'How do you feel this morning?'

'Good.' He felt tired.

'So do I.' Marie paused to gulp something. She avoided caffeine and citrus fruits. 'Listen. I usually take Miriam to the pet store on Saturday. But Goshe wants me to work today. Would you mind very much taking her? You still have to get a heater anyway, don't you?'

'I do. And no, I don't mind at all. I'd like to.'

'Excellent. That'll make her happy.' She lowered her voice and Ken could hear the dampened clinks of plates in water. 'Last night was good for me. Let's do it again.'

'We will.'

Miriam was waiting out in front of the house on the Beach Road. Small in the passenger seat, she watched the passing streets and houses. Ken felt a warm contentment. A completed pleasure: nothing more needed or asked for.

They looked at the iguanas, inert, with slivering tongues. At the turtles clambering at slippery rocks. The new rabbits, squirming, dung-smeared. Family life, Ken thought, not unhappily. Mr Hecht with his dirty fingernails and food between his teeth, the same checked shirt.

Miriam seemed proud to be able to name the fish – 'There's the danio … there's the moor' – and unbothered by the discrepancy between the store's brighter, more active versions and her own. Was she even aware of it? Ken was surprised when she pointed at a shrimp behind a rock and said, with her partial smile, 'Jumbo.'

After he had paid for the heater and thermometer, she slid a pet diary onto the counter, along with a small pile of change.

On the way to the car, Miriam thrust the book at Ken in a child's impulsive gesture.

'Thank you,' he said thickly, too touched to say more.

They went to McDonald's on the way home. Miriam ate her Big Mac slowly, looking around at the bustle and the lime-green décor, seemingly bored by Ken's awkward speculations about what fish he might start with. A blankness came over him, a profound boredom that he was not free to acknowledge.

Family life, he thought.

The rest of the weekend was tense, constrained by the awareness that he was not calling Marie. Was he being unfair in assuming that she expected him to? The phone stared at him.

Only after midnight Sunday did he feel his time become his own again. The work week. Free of expectations and full of excuses.

From the futon – moving to the other bed hadn't been necessary, after all – he stared up at the illuminated tank. Yellow, bubbling water, frilled and backed by green fronds, topped with the warm black of the window, night pressing from the other side.

He had to remind himself that this image, which seemed perfect already, was insufficient, that it needed the fish, feeding and excreting and dying, that he would begin adding in a week.

He got a pen and opened the pet diary Miriam had given him. What he wrote seemed more like an invocation than Sondra's 'character research'. He thought so afterwards, trying to classify the few sentences. The words themselves came without effort.

Miriam at Bedtime

The covers are pulled up to her shoulders. Her pyjamas are pink and white, with small shapes that might be roses. Her hands are folded as if in prayer, her thumbs slightly parted to hold the book. Her dark hair has not been washed in a day or two, oil darkens it, and her face is very serious. Her mouth open slightly over crooked teeth.

It was nothing like Sondra's various productions: inner journey journals, dream landscapes, dialogues with her animus, interrogations of her dead parents. It wasn't a conscientious work-up of character motivation. *Why does R shout at S in Act II? He is remembering Clara.* What, then?

He closed the book and turned off the aquarium light. The water temperature was holding steady now at 24 degrees Celsius, within the safe range.

On Tuesday evening Miriam phoned. Ken picked up the phone with trepidation and heard a small, distant, expressionless voice. Like a voice in a tin can. Or a seashell.

'Jumbo shed his skin.'

'He did?'

'At first we thought he was sick. He went sort of white.'

'How do you know he shed his skin?'

'It's there.'

'His skin?'

'The old one.'

He was curious to see it, but it was out of the question to arrive at the Evers' apartment for that reason alone.

'Keep me posted,' he said lamely, after a long silence. Then, worse, he added, 'Say hi to your mother for me.'

On Thursday, ashamed of his continued silence, he forced himself to visit Marie at Words. Her blank face looked preliminary, as if the furniture had been pushed into the corners to make room.

Soon, but not so quickly that it seemed like atonement, he invited her to dinner Saturday. He said 'you', having been unable to decide whether it was best to invite Miriam or not. He would leave it up to her.

'Saturday? That sounds fine,' she said coolly.

He relaxed a bit. He had expected to pay for the past week.

By the way she manoeuvred herself into Rombo's a few minutes later, banging her canes against the chairs, he gathered more payment was due. Very quickly, he saw what form it would take. His asking after Miriam led to parenthood led to sullen memories of Marie's father, an abusive logger in B.C. where she had grown up. When he made sympathetic comments, her mouth, the soft mouth he had kissed too hard, drooped. He couldn't win. And when she stopped, he had no comparable tale to tell.

'Who was your father?'

'My father?' He shrugged. 'A sport fisherman who claimed never to dream.'

She nodded sombrely. Miriam's father used to take her fishing on Lake Joseph.

It was happening again. He was the privileged one. He had had his parental spats and griefs, but he had gone past them, years ago, to conclude that something had simply failed to happen between his parents and himself, something that he wished had happened, and which perhaps should have. A universal condition, a hard pill. He had swallowed it, adjusted, as he had parcelled out his severance cheque to augment his UI benefits. But Marie was still gimping along, flailing into Words and into the sad past.

'You're different,' she said morosely.

No, he thought. Not the role of tender freak: the one good man. It was a hapless one. He was a man, damn it; not drunk and enraged, but surely not harmless. He wished he could run.

To change the subject, he inquired about Jumbo. Marie related that after his skin change he was noticeably larger and stronger. He climbed the water like a cyclist, dove hard. She related this like evidence. All themes were one.

'See you Saturday,' she said, payment past, or deferred.

From the corner he watched her, squat and teetering, flail towards her car. The canes flashed in the sun like swords.

Saturday morning, despite a long sleep, he woke with sore joints and a logy, bruised feeling, as though soft fists had pummelled him. Each day was a lottery. Plunging his arms into the aquarium, before he was fully awake, was no help; the water was warm.

Marie arrived at six, alone. When he heard her coming, he left the door open and got busy at the sink. He wanted to avoid turning around just yet – though who better to understand than she?

'I'm afraid I have some bad news,' she said, from behind him. 'Jumbo died.'

'How?'

'Who knows? We found him legs up this morning.' Was she baiting him with this chipper voice?

'I hope Miriam wasn't too upset.'

'Well, she was disappointed, of course. But she's had to put a lot of x's in her diary. They don't last. She knows that.'

He turned stiffly. Marie had cut her hair and streaked it with silver. She was wearing a turtleneck and blazer that gave her a little more verticality. She looked like she had the first time he had seen her: alluring, independent.

But in the instant he was admiring her, she saw his face and exclaimed, 'Oh! Bad day?'

Nodding, he felt his eyes fill.

She came to him and brushed the bumps on his nose and cheeks with her cool thumbs. 'What are you doing at the sink? Come with me.'

And, though she had never been to his apartment before, she led him down the hall to the bedroom. 'Lie down.' She went back up the hall and came back with the dish towel filled with ice cubes. Climbing awkwardly over him to the other side, she unbuttoned his shirt and began gently rubbing him down with the cool damp cloth.

The relief it brought was amazing. He closed his eyes. Soon she was easing his clothes off. She did not ignore his face, his bare scalp, his feet (which tickled), or his groin. She asked him to turn over, and when he did, she passed the now dripping cloth repeatedly down over his back and buttocks and down the length of his legs. He heard her own joints crackling in protest at the movements she was making.

She asked him again to turn over. He did so, keeping his eyes closed. With excitement he heard a clacking of ice cubes followed by the wet plop of the towel onto the floor. Then her mouth was on him. He gasped at the thrilling cold, the cold rocks in pockets of warmth sliding up and down him. After a few shivering passes, he had to signal with his fingers on her head that he was ready. But she kept her mouth on him while he came, jetting like a squid.

For some moments he basked in the cessation of all pain.

'My God ... thank you,' he whispered.

'You have no idea what can be done,' she said.

After a while, she showed him how to do a little more. She asked for extra pillows, and when he brought them from the closet, she positioned them in a row behind each of them, then turned herself around so that they could go down on each other in comfort. Lounging on his side, tonguing her at his leisure, he felt like Tiberius at a banquet. It seemed almost too easy, sex reduced to frictionless exchange. Yet it worked better for them. What would they use on the worst days? Vibrators and gel? Surrogates?

The pain returned when he went back to fixing dinner but his greater relaxation helped him bear it better. You could ride the pain on a wave, sometimes. He snipped a cupful of basil leaves for the pesto sauce. Marie was lying on the futon, reading.

The atmosphere could not have been better calculated so that what happened next took him completely by surprise.

They had been talking around the divider about Monday, his start-up day. How Miriam might get a kick out of helping him pick the fish. They stopped talking as he whirred the leaves and garlic in his blender. Suddenly, as he was spooning in yoghurt, he heard a series of brusque sounds. He looked behind him. Marie had her blazer on and her canes in one hand, the other on the doorknob.

'Marie. What...?' He put his hand on her arm to detain her. She shook it away; it hurt him, and must have hurt her. The canes in her other hand banged the wall.

He followed her down the hall a few steps, sputtering, 'Marie ... Tell me ...' then stopped and watched her go. A suspicion flew into his head, paralysing him. Marie's motion, on the other hand, shooting canes and pumping legs, seemed to fill the hall.

He waited until he heard her car start, then went back inside. He looked around the divider. On the floor lay the open pet diary. *Miriam at Bedtime.* What would Marie, what would any mother, make of it?

* * *

Although he did not expect to see Marie again, he was resolved to try to explain himself. He stayed up late trying to compose a letter and ripping up the efforts, most of them no more than introductory phrases. *Marie, I know what you must be.* . . .

It was no use. It was too innocent, or too unknown, to explain. An image of Miriam had bubbled up; he had taken it down. That didn't explain anything.

After a while he was urging, rather than promising, himself to do it; and, more often, worrying about how he would react to meeting her on the street; rueing the fact that Words was closed to him now. Anger surfaced amid his regret. Anger at Marie. What business did she have opening his journal? Anger at the smashed logger, taking his hatred of the forest out on his wife's face. Anger at Sondra. Her writing was always a 'learning experience' because it never surprised her. She hadn't been nurtured. Well, who had?

When he finally went to bed, he couldn't sleep. His knees and elbows were fiery. The pump sounded like approaching aircraft. What a fucking stupid idea!

He limped down the hall to the other room, but turned back at the sight of the double lines of pillows, like sandbags arranged for point blank warfare. He yanked the pump plug out of the socket and collapsed on the futon.

At some point he must have fallen asleep, because he felt himself rise from some deeper state to a half-dreaming level where he heard shuffling, rasping noises. Something in a cage was trying to get out. Digging or pacing. Rubbing. Bangs, as of the animal lunging at its bars, brought him fully awake, and he heard a car drive up.

It was dark.

He plugged in the aquarium light and the pump, then turned the other lights on. When the knocking came, a soft tapping near the floor, somehow he wasn't surprised.

Along with dismay, he felt a surge of déjà vu at seeing Marie sitting with her back to the wall, her legs splayed and her damp head lowered. Sondra had done something very similar for the bereavment scene in *The Sea Bride*. Right down to the hollow voice.

'I left Miriam alone. I've never done that before. But I can't talk to you if you won't answer your door.'

'I was asleep.'

She nodded, and raised herself with difficulty. 'Can I come in for a minute?'

'Of course.'

Inside, she looked about carefully, as if seeing the apartment for the first time. 'I don't like people who run off. They're like people who don't call. They leave people wondering.' She shot him a glance. 'So I came back.'

He nodded grimly. He wanted to take his lumps and get this over with.

'First off, I'm curious. No. Stop.' She cancelled what she was about to say. 'Listen, Ken, I'm sure there are lots of things we'd both like to say about earlier. I hope we get the chance. But I wanted you to know that I don't think you're a pervert.'

He gulped in relief. But along with the relief, highlighting it, was a flicker of disappointment. It was too soon to understand it.

Marie went on. 'I know why you want to think of a little girl in bed. At least I think I do. It's because it's a pure good. And you're right. It is pure. And it is good. But, Ken, it's only a beginning. It's like your aquarium. It's a start. Do you know what I'm saying?'

He nodded, but he wasn't sure.

Marie opened her mouth, then, searching his face, suddenly seemed too tired to talk any more. They stood in silence. Her navy blazer and the plum circles under her wide-set eyes glowed with the backlit clarity of an illumination in stained glass.

She stuck out her hand. 'Take care of yourself.'

Then she retrieved her canes from outside the door where she had left them and made off down the hall.

Let off, let down. In the silence after Marie left, Ken understood the treachery of the words for the first time. None of the things he had braced himself for – shouting in the streets, vicious rumours – would happen. Pillows had been rearranged. The aquarium had been given one of Miriam's semi-cleanings and the bodies ticked off as still swimming.

Washing the dishes – an old adjustment strategy – he found himself wondering what the Players were working on these days. They didn't phone any more. After becoming too ill to strut and fret, he had lost all interest in contributing in other ways, refusing invitations to serve as set designer, script collaborator, prompter. Marg Soames had sewn costumes for every production for the last fifteen years, while coping with an alcoholic husband and, latterly, her own cancer. But he would rather stay alone on a sickbed, a futon with a milk-crate hassock, than be the plucky guy with lupus at the cast party, hugged too hard by actors still on an adrenaline rush. Sondra had seen the light, and gone the way of the coated rose.

He shivered suddenly, thinking of that dreamless angler, his father. His hands lowered a plate into soapy water.

I don't expect to hear from you. After twenty years, the mild voice still echoed, no fainter than it had been on the day he had left home. A terrible prediction, any way it got sliced. Fail-safe.

He made himself a tea and sat down on the chair beside the futon to watch the sky lighten. The empty aquarium babbled like an idiot, frothing at the mouth. Dawn came, pink and grey.

He picked up the pet diary and tore out the offending page. He ripped it into small pieces. Anxious to make them vanish, he told himself to wait until he was heading past the garbage can anyway. Motion had to be conserved, especially in the absence of adequate rest. Marie understood that. He hadn't, but he was beginning to.

On the clean page of the diary Miriam had given him, under the date, he copied, distractedly, the sample first entry that had been provided for young pet owners:

Tomorrow my system will be ready to sustain life.

The Leading Edge

THE OPENING WAS OVER. Up in the lounge, volunteers worked to clear away the plastic wine glasses, paper plates, and cheese and fruit platters. Some of the lights were off; before the motion detectors could be turned on I had to walk through the art gallery and make sure all the patrons had gone. As I exited each room, I said its name into my walkie-talkie. Down in the basement, the man working the security panel armed the alarm. In a job of often killing boredom, it was one of my favourite duties. Myself in motion, the leading edge of security, leaving peace and stillness behind me.

I left the small gallery of contemporary art, at the back of the building, until the last. It was where I usually found them.

He was standing in the centre of the room, looking at his drawings. It was odd to approach him from behind, since all of his pencil drawings were of the backs of people. He was a precise draughtsman; all around the grey walls, people, about life-size, sat or stood with their backs to us.

He turned at the sound of my footsteps on the hardwood floor.

'Close up?'

'No hurry.'

He was a tall, thin man wearing glasses and a cardigan. Limp grey hair fell down towards one eye. According to the catalogue, a pile of which sat on a pedestal in the corner, he had sold his work privately and in juried exhibitions, but this was his first one-man show.

'I like your drawings.'

His eyes opened wider; that was all.

'Take your time,' I said, backing away. I didn't mind waiting a few minutes in the lobby, where I had a chess game going over walkie-talkie with the security panel guard. But then I remembered something I should tell this artist. One thing I had learned about artists, in four years working here: they seldom had any idea what people really thought about their work. Standing in my uniform by a wall, quiet as a beige statue, I overheard people's reactions. I told the artists what I thought they'd like to hear. They were usually very interested.

'People wonder something about your drawings,' I said, coming back to him.

'Oh?'

'They wonder if you know what the people look like.'

His eyebrows rose, two pencil smears.

'Some people say that you must use models, so of course you know their faces. Other people say that, since you're just drawing them from behind, it doesn't matter what they look like.'

'They say this?' He had an accent. Europe, somewhere.

'Yes.'

It wasn't all they said. They also said his art was brilliant, it was a waste of paper, it captured the alienation of modern life, it forced the viewer to be interactive by extrapolating from a few cues. But these were not the kinds of comments I felt I could relay. I focused on smaller, to me more interesting, things.

'Come here,' the artist said. He moved a little closer to one wall and I followed him.

'Tell me what you see,' he said.

I looked at the two drawings hung side by side in front of us. Each was about two feet wide by three high, framed in black.

'Go ahead,' he said.

So I did.

'I see two men sitting in wooden chairs,' I said. 'An older man and a younger one. There could be a breeze blowing because some of their hairs are out of place. They're both wearing sweaters.'

'What else?'

I hesitated. I wasn't usually asked for my own observations. I wasn't sure how far to go.

Then I said, 'I would say they're both very interested in what they're seeing. They seem to be leaning forward slightly.'

There was a pause while he considered my words. I could feel cool currents from the air conditioning. Up high in one corner, a security camera pointed down at us. If the guard was watching, he would be getting impatient; he took his chess seriously.

'You don't see,' the artist said. Disappointment sharpened his accent.

'What?'

He gestured, making sketching motions in the air. 'Look at their necks and backs. The muscles and weight have shifted. Just slightly. No one seems to see it,' he said, his voice tinged with bitterness, 'but all of my people have just started to turn.'

I continued looking at the two drawings. Peering at the pencil marks, trying to see the difference he claimed. I *could* see it, of course, now that he'd told me, but I couldn't be sure if I was just imagining it. With more courage, I might have asked him which way they were turning.

'Maybe I don't have enough knowledge of anatomy,' I said finally.

'Maybe,' he agreed.

We stood there. Not saying anything else. My walkie-talkie made a burp of static. It was my chess partner, signalling for a move. The artist moved a little way off, closer to another of his pictures. I signalled back that I'd heard, then switched the walkie-talkie off.

What the artist had said changed things, there was no doubt about that. I had been looking at a bunch of backs and necks and haircuts, but now I had to imagine that I was about to meet some people. Movement came into the equation. It was almost a sound I could hear; like the shiftings of a theatre audience in the dark, only quieter. Like the tissuey whisper of the angel wings in the Old Master room upstairs, when it was just you and the oil paintings, near closing time.

Dr Lekky's Rose

PAUL WAS ON HIS WAY into the liquor store when he heard a small, bright sound. *Chip. Chip.* He looked up. A little above him, large white letters spelling LIQUOR CONTROL BOARD projected from the brick wall. Inside the O in LIQUOR, a sparrow was sitting on an untidy nest, chirping. It looked down at him, switching its head from side to side. When it opened its beak the bright sound sprang out. Other letters – the C, the B and D – had bits of sticks and dried grass stuck in them, the beginnings or remains of other nests.

Why not? he thought. Birds usually didn't interest him much, but he was new to the neighbourhood and he was still noticing everything. He stood for a few moments longer, the April sun glittering all around him. But then he thought he might be frightening the bird – its head was flicking faster now – and he went inside.

Out of habit, he got a cart and started pulling bottles down as he walked slowly down the aisles. Vodka. Scotch. Gin. Red and white wine. He was headed for the cooler with the cans of imported beer, when he suddenly stopped and thought: Think.

Think, he told himself, standing behind the cart.

He went back up the aisles he had come down, replacing the bottles carefully. They felt slippery in his hand and he kept his other hand near the bottom of each bottle as it moved through the air.

The Gordon's gin was all he kept. It felt warm enough for a summer drink. After he paid for it, he went into Catelli's, the Italian grocery store next door. Check out the bearded lady, Jean had said when she came back from buying cigarettes yesterday.

Standing in line with his limes and tonic water, and the groceries Jean had requested, Paul saw who she meant. The cashier was a big Italian woman, maybe forty, with a large black mole beside her mouth. She had bristles on her upper lip and dark fluff on her cheeks. She was speaking in Italian to an old man who was fumbling for his change. His fingers shook as he poked at the coins in his palm.

Then the cashier reached over and began picking out the coins

31

she needed. The old man held out his cupped palm and let her. They both kept speaking in Italian. Paul had to smile as he watched them. The little old man was about half her size.

Out on the deck of their third-floor apartment, he told Jean about spotting the first crocus of the season. There weren't many flowers he could identify by name, but crocuses he knew. Twenty years ago, his first girlfriend had liked to point them out to him, along with other signs of spring. *Listen to the robins.* He'd heard her soft voice again as he stood for a moment on the sidewalk, watching a blue tip poke through the neighbour's lawn.

'Gin?' Jean said, looking in the paper bag.

He knew she meant *Just gin?*, but he answered, 'Sure. Get summer started.'

Jean looked up at him from her kitchen chair, most of her face hidden behind a wide-brimmed floppy hat and oversize sunglasses. *My Toronto look*, she'd called it, as if anonymity needed a further coating of disguise. She took out her DuMauriers and lit one, slowly. Paul measured the defeat of his own smoking habit by the way he could watch this calmly now. Not feeling angry any more that she hadn't stopped with him, at most only a dim resentment that she still enjoyed it so obviously. She tilted her head back to exhale, the wrinkles in her neck smoothing away.

He took the two bags back through the sliding glass door into the narrow kitchen. He put the meat and vegetables in the fridge, the tonic water and gin in the freezer. They hadn't made ice yet, neither of them remembering where they had packed the trays. He looked out into the living room where most of their life was still piled in boxes. Alleys, or tunnels, led through the boxes to the bathroom and the bedroom. Mr Rice, their landlord, had helped them carry some of it up the stairs yesterday. They unpacked enough to get the bedroom functional, and the bathroom and kitchen, then ate takeout chicken and drank a bottle of wine they'd brought in a cooler. Jean didn't ask for anything else when the bottle was empty. They were both exhausted.

He checked his watch: 5:45. He wrestled another kitchen chair out from a tangle of furniture and joined Jean outside.

They sat near the railing, looking out over the back yards. So this was Toronto. The yards were small, and in this neighbourhood most of the space was given over to gardening. Two houses over, a man with a shovel was turning earth. Another yard had a grape arbour, the dried vines scrolling over it.

'That must be our winemaker,' Paul said. Mr Rice had mentioned bottles of rosé, a tasting party.

'What?' Jean said.

He repeated what he had said. After that they sat in silence.

At the stroke of six, he looked at his watch and said, 'Well, I guess it might be time for refreshments.'

After two drinks, Jean took her sunglasses off. He saw her greenish eyes again, the fine white lines like rays around them. 'These are a good summer drink, aren't they?' she said.

'Only the best.'

'Do you think you could make me another one? Soon?'

'I'll make you one *forthwith*.'

She smiled. For a moment, it felt like any other day.

They had met five years ago, in Orillia, Jean's home town. Paul had gone there to be with a woman, and when that ended, had stayed on. He fell in with a loose collection of people that met most nights at one of three bars. It was a large enough group that the time and place never had to be specified. If you showed up at one of these bars, anytime after 4 p.m., some of the people would be there. Others would drift in later.

They called themselves the PTA – Part-Timers Association – because of the number of them who worked at part-time jobs. It was the economy, they said. And it was true that was part of it.

One night when there was a country-rock band playing at the Star Motel, the PTA took over the dance floor, and Paul found himself dancing near a woman with a good figure in a short black leather skirt. She was swaying to the beat with her eyes closed, ash-blond hair falling across her face. She opened her eyes once and registered who was in front of her, then shut them again.

One look told Paul that she was electric, somebody with the power to make things happen. He hadn't known many such people in his life, and he was sure that he wasn't one himself.

The next song was a slow one. He opened his arms and she stepped inside them, snuggling close against his chest. They hugged each other and shuffled in a slow circle. The two dances, and the contrast between them, had Paul's heart pounding.

When the set ended, they sat down at one of the PTA tables. They told each other their first names. They ordered two new drinks and didn't talk again until they came. After a sip, Jean asked, 'So, how do you survive?'

It was a common PTA question, and Paul had a set answer. He worked twenty hours a week at a video store. Time meant more to him than money, and he knew how to budget. He was single, never-married.

He also told Jean something he didn't usually mention until he knew someone better. Some women he'd dated had never known it. 'Also,' he said, 'my parents left me some money. That's my play fund.' He raised his glass.

Jean raised hers.

'What about you?' he asked.

'My husband left me his house,' she said.

Shortly after that, while Jean was in the washroom, another PTA member named Donna sat down on the other side of Paul. He'd caught her eye while he'd been dancing with Jean. Donna and he had gone out for a while, years back. She'd been plump then; now she was fat. When the others had gotten up to dance she'd stayed at the table, drinking.

'How's things?' Paul asked.

'Could be worse,' Donna said. 'Anytime I start feeling sorry for myself, I remind myself that I've never come home and found my husband hanging in the basement.'

'What?' Paul said.

Donna rolled her eyes toward the washroom. 'Jean Prentiss.'

At the sound of Jean's last name, Paul remembered the newspaper story. It had been talked about a lot for a while. *Can you imagine....* Everyone could and couldn't.

'I thought you'd take a husband hanging anywhere,' he said to Donna.

Donna smiled sweetly at him. 'Fuck off,' she said.

In a little while, Paul looked over the railing and saw Mr Rice down in the yard. He was strolling around, looking at various plants and bushes, and the small tree that he'd already told them was a peach tree. He seemed to be taking stock after the winter.

The landlord looked up and waved. Paul waved back.

'Mr Rice seems to want to talk to me,' he told Jean. 'I'll be back up in a minute.'

What he didn't say was that the sight of the other man checking his plants had made him feel claustrophobic all of a sudden, perched up here with Jean. Besides, it was time to give Jean a try on her own. He didn't want this to turn into a case of constant surveillance. No couple could stand that.

Jean didn't say anything.

On his way past the kitchen, Paul noted the level of the gin by the letters on the side of the Gordon's bottle. Top of the O.

Down in the yard, he and Mr Rice shook hands, as they had last night and also the other time they'd met, when Paul looked at and paid for the apartment. Mr Rice was a tiny man, a widower with a pale, pinched face. In his rubber boots and old plaid jacket he seemed to be dressed for yard work, though there were no implements in sight.

'Settling in?' he said, his voice high for a man.

'Getting there,' Paul replied.

'It takes time. Course, we've had the house twenty years, but I don't know how many addresses we had before that.' Mr Rice spoke as if his wife were still alive, part of a *we* still active in the world. Paul hadn't heard her name yet.

'Hello up there.' Mr Rice shielded his eyes with his hands as he called up. Paul tilted his head back. Jean was leaning against the black wrought iron railing, wreathed in smoke, with her hat and magnum shades, one hand raised.

'Fine-looking woman,' Mr Rice said, lowering his hand and voice.

'Thank you,' said Paul, who had been thinking Jean looked bizarre.

'Reminds me of Greta Garbo. Or the Queen, you know that way she has of waving from that balcony.'

'Yes,' Paul said.

'How old are you two, if you don't mind my asking?'

'I'm thirty-nine and Jean is forty-nine,' Paul answered. He didn't try to fudge the gap anymore; Jean never had. Five years ago, people had often expressed disbelief that she was over forty. That hadn't happened in a while. Time had caught up with her, or she with it.

'Couple of big ones coming,' Mr Rice said. When Paul didn't respond, he added, 'Fifty and forty.' He moved away across the lawn, chuckling. 'Course, I'd take either one and feel like a spring chicken. First night in a new place,' he said, Paul following him uncertainly, 'Mrs Rice would be down on her knees in her kerchief and dungarees, scrubbing the floors so we could eat off them. Spraying Lysol.'

The landlord stopped abruptly, as if on the verge of something. Paul stopped too, beside and a little behind him.

'That round table leaning against the fence,' Mr Rice pointed into a corner by a shed. 'It belongs to the third floor, if you want it. Some chairs in the shed too. Dr Lekky left them here.'

'Dr Lekky?'

'The previous tenant. In your place. Didn't I mention him?'

Paul tried to remember. 'I don't think so,' he said.

'Well, anyway, that's his rose too.' Mr Rice pointed to a cluster of thorned stalks sticking out of a low mound of earth in front of the fence. 'Give the bulb another couple of weeks to warm up and you're welcome to it. Your wife might like it.'

Jean wasn't his wife, but Paul didn't correct the landlord. He was confused by something else, some cloudiness in his head. 'We could get a pot, I guess,' he said.

Mr Rice grinned up at him like a leprechaun. 'The pot's in the ground. Buried. All you have to do is dig it up.'

'The pot's buried?' Paul stared at the mound of earth, picturing it.

'Sure,' said Mr Rice with his sly grin, 'Best insulation in the world. Earth and clay and earth. Triple protection. No way the bulb can freeze. That's what I told Dr Lekky. He wanted to keep it inside all winter.' Mr Rice shook his head in amazement. 'You ever hear of keeping a rose inside?'

'No,' Paul said. Though he didn't see anything ridiculous in it either. He didn't garden.

On his way up the stairs, he wondered what circumstances had led to a doctor living in a third-floor walk-up. Two or three possibilities came to mind, none of them good. No one was safe; that was the truth of it. He wanted Mr Rice to tell him, but then he didn't too. Where was Dr Lekky now? He imagined Mr Rice telling him the story some summer night.

Upstairs, Jean had started making the stew. She was cutting up carrots and celery to add to the pressure cooker, her cigarette ash drooping precariously as she chopped. The gin bottle and the glasses were not in sight. Paul was sorry he couldn't check the bottle right now, but the grim set of Jean's face as she chopped the vegetables, the knife click-clicking on the cutting board, had the effect of reassuring him. She would have been more relaxed if she'd gone past their three-drink limit. Sometimes they used to straggle up to dinner at ten, when, laughing and indifferent, one of them would scramble eggs or warm up soup.

Sitting in a chair by the sliding door, he told her about Dr Lekky's rose as he watched her fix dinner. He embellished the story a bit, the way it was already growing in his own mind, saying that Dr Lekky couldn't get over not having a yard. He was worried about what would happen to his potted rose.

'So worried he left it behind,' Jean murmured. Paul was almost certain she'd been good.

They had lived for four years in the house left to Jean by her husband, the suicide who had killed himself out of the blue. No warning, no note. He had left a little money too, but Jean also worked part-time at the library.

Having late-morning jobs – Paul's shift started at eleven and Jean's at noon – made one less obstacle to drinking late at night. Drinking was a large part of their life, it was what they mainly did together. They drank and sat, they drank and made love, they drank and talked. Cold sober, neither of them was much of a talker, but after a drink or two, they could open up and discuss their lives as if they were drifting over them in a balloon, pointing out old sights. *I tried to hold him up by his legs, to take the weight off, but I had to let go to phone 911.*

They even talked about drinking less; it came up along with everything else.

Another thing they talked about sometimes was finding full-time jobs before their nest eggs ran out and they got too old for anyone to take a chance on. Moving to Toronto was part of this fresh-start scenario. The Big Smoke, Paul would say, blowing a perfect smoke ring. This was before he quit.

One morning, Paul found a hand-delivered letter in the mailbox. It was a plain white envelope with his name typed on the front. No stamp, no address.

He opened it outside the door and read the typed message:

JEAN DRINKS AT WORK. FROM A FRIEND.

He didn't show Jean. She was still sleeping. She drank a little less than he did on average, but her hangovers were worse.

When the video store was empty that afternoon, he phoned Donna. He and Jean no longer went to PTA meetings, but he knew that Donna had gotten married and that she and her husband were in twelve-step. He also remembered her reading detective novels. It was his best shot.

'Where can we meet?' he said when Donna answered the phone.

She named a restaurant near the video store.

'Okay,' Paul said. 'Three-fifteen.' Quitting time.

'Nice to see you, Paul.' Donna had lost a little weight and she had rinsed the grey out of her hair.

'Let's have it,' he said. If some gossip was starting up, he wanted to stamp it out fast.

But Donna simply looked at him, saying nothing. The waitress came and Donna ordered a coffee. Paul ordered a beer.

Donna looked away, then back at him. 'Please don't be angry at me, Paul. I'm just telling you the facts.'

'What are your facts?' he said.

Donna sighed. 'Ed warned me you wouldn't want to hear it.' Ed was her husband.

'What are your facts?'

'Okay. I'm telling you.' She paused and went on evenly. 'A few days ago, the librarian let me use the staff washroom. When I went in, I saw Jean standing in the stall, drinking from a bottle. I backed out again, but I'm sure she saw me.'

Paul saw the tawdry picture bloom in his mind, took a sort of mental step towards it, and then backed away quietly, as Donna had. Closed the door.

The waitress came with his beer and Donna's coffee. Paul tipped his beer back and drank half of it. Donna was looking down at her coffee. After a few moments, she said, 'I'll leave now, Paul. I know the score. Believe me, I do. It's up to Jean and you. All I'm going to say is that Jean needs to start the program, now. The other thing I'll say is that she'll never do it alone. Ed and I learned that the hard way. Why do you think I talked to you, not Jean?'

Paul felt his chest tighten. He thought that if Donna didn't leave in a moment he would hit her, go across the table at her. Luckily, she stood up.

'This wasn't easy for me,' she said. 'I knew how you'd probably take it.'

'Right,' he said.

Donna backed away.

'You've lost weight,' he said, smiling.

By the time Jean got home that night, he had it all mapped out. The number of drinks, the time of day they could start, the rewards for good behaviour. The program. Their program.

Control.

Jean watched him as he laid it out, with her head in three-quarter profile to him, her eyes directed out into the living room yet at the same time watching him minutely. Her posture was the oddest thing to him then. It was like a Cubist painting, a Picasso head, that sheers away and faces you at the same time.

She didn't cry. Paul had never seen her cry except from laughing. She didn't protest or even ask questions. That was what made what Donna said she had seen in the bathroom come back into his mind and lodge there, true. But he didn't mention it to Jean. Or the word *alcoholic*. What he said, and he believed this, was that they were social drinkers who had gone too far.

'Another thing,' he said, 'we can't do it here. We know everybody. Everybody knows us.'

Jean sat silently.

'In Toronto we'll be two more specks. And there's bound to be more jobs there.'

She still didn't say anything. Was she waiting for six o'clock? Already?

'It'll mean apartment living at first. Housing prices there are crazy. But once we start working we should have enough for a down payment on something.' He heard his voice rising, and stopped. But then he put his hands together like a preacher, as if he were playing a part. 'I guess even a good thing can get out of hand.' Jean's head was sinking slowly.

'If you think this is too hard, say so,' he said.

She flashed him a glance that took his breath away. It was like forked lightning, twin bolts of violent green that fused in a single scornful question.

Too hard? Too hard?

Just for an instant, and then her eyes clouded over, leaving only the afterimage of a storm in his mind.

He lay on his side in bed, unable to sleep. He closed his eyes but he had an unpleasant sensation of spinning slowly, as if a carnival ride were starting up. When he opened his eyes he saw the bedroom wall. *My bedroom wall.* How many other people had called it that? Had got undressed, set their alarms?

He and Jean had gone to bed at ten o'clock. The night seemed very long. They didn't have new routines to fill it yet. He saw that they would have to find some, and soon.

Around midnight, the scratching sounds began. Digging and scratching, something with claws. It came from somewhere up above them, where the roof met the wall. The sounds would stop, then start again.

Behind him he could feel Jean still awake. 'Squirrels?' he said. 'Raccoons?' He used the plural even though he only heard one animal.

'Bastards,' Jean muttered. 'Better call Rice and get him up here with a cage.'

Paul chuckled at the thought. He put out his hand under the covers and found Jean's warm hip. It felt slightly clammy, filmed with moisture. He patted her and drew his hand back.

'I thought autumn was supposed to be the time they tried to get into houses. Looking for winter homes. In spring they should be headed outside.' He remembered the sparrows nesting in the letters and thought of another reason an animal would be looking for a refuge.

There was a long pause, several minutes, then it started again. Scrabble, scrabble, scrabble. Tiny, furious paws.

'Maybe it's Dr Lucky,' she said.

'Dr Lekky?'

'Lucky ... lecky....?' She sounded so tired. He had to listen carefully to hear the charge, her current, underneath the tiredness. But he could still hear it. A hum.

'Coming through the roof?' he said.

'Coming to get his rose.'

Soon after that, the pawing stopped, and little feet went away across the shingles.

He woke up out of a dream that was not like his usual dreams. He didn't dream often, at least not that he remembered, and when he did his dreams were bizarre and fragmented – filled with muddled voices, flashes of people and animals, sometimes people turning into animals. Nothing that made much sense. It was like someone ran a story through a blender, and he was looking at it as it whirled.

This dream was different. It seemed real enough to be happening. He thought he was awake. The Italian woman in the grocery store, the hairy cashier, was picking change out of his palm. Speaking in Italian to him. He was nodding and smiling. He knew it was important not to speak, not to let her know that they spoke different languages. If he did, he knew that she would say something coarse and dismissive. *Asshole. You're a tourist.* Something like that.

She got what she needed, and shut the cash register drawer. He woke up.

A sound. A real sound. Not a dream.

He moved his arm sideways a bit, farther. She wasn't there.

'Jean?' he called. No answer. But he thought he heard a cupboard door close, something splash in a glass.

With a stumbling heart, he made his way between the stacks of boxes toward the lighted kitchen. Jean was leaning back against the counter in her plaid housecoat, drinking something clear from a glass.

'Thirsty?' he said.

'Mm.' She drank. 'Little buggers kept me up.'

'Really? I didn't hear them.'

'You were dead.'

He watched her drink. Need is cunning, he thought. Cunning and need: they're aspects of the same thing. But Jean was struggling, he knew that. Could you ask more from a person?

Yes, he thought. You had to.

'I'm thirsty too,' he said.

'Want some?' she said, her eyes flicking at him before she extended the glass. Not quite close enough to smell, but the gesture was enough for Paul. He got a glass from the cupboard and ran water into it. The sound was the same. What he had heard.

The sun came up behind the houses like a red bulb pushing through the soil. They were sitting on the chairs on the deck. They hadn't been able to sleep again so they'd put on their jackets and come out here. Jean had wiped the dew off both chairs with her sleeve. She was smoking and Paul was dying for one. It would be a year next month and he hadn't felt cravings like this since the first week.

'I'm going to get my sunglasses,' Jean said when the sun was only a little higher. Paul could still look right into it.

He sat in the cool moist air, shivering, wanting a smoke. This is the program, he thought. All the rest of it, the six months since he'd talked to Donna – selling the house, apartment-hunting, saying goodbye to friends – that was just getting ready for it. No surprise there. He was the one who'd said they had to be in a completely different place for anything to really change. And he still believed that. The PTA had thrown a farewell party and they'd gotten smashed.

Smashed. They'd kept on having the same drinks before dinner. It had only felt different because they were so much busier during the day. Getting ready. Moving.

He knew all that. It was just a shock to see that this was only the start. Everything – everything – was still ahead of them.

Jean came back with a plate with two English muffins, toasted, with butter and jam. 'So, when's the big job search start?' she said.

'I'll buy a paper today,' he said. Thinking: Christ, forty.

'That's how you do it?' He was looking out over the railing, but he could hear the smile in her voice.

'It's a start,' he said.

'Reading the ads?'

'*Studying* them.'

They both crunched their English muffins.

'It might be nice to have a little rose bush up here, what do you think?' She sounded peppy, almost perky now. It occurred to Paul that it could work that way, one of them supporting the other, then being supported. Trading places.

'Sure,' he said. But inside, he was thinking that Dr Lekky's rose sounded more like bad luck than good. Who needed a flower that someone had stuck in the ground and then forgotten? What good could come of it?

She flicked her cigarette over the railing.

'Hey,' he said. 'We live here.'

Jean said something back to him, but he didn't catch it because he was watching the butt go spinning end over end down to the grass. It had already landed but he could still see it falling, like a scene on video loop. There was a good inch left beyond the filter. He would have to go down in a minute and pick it up, before Mr Rice found it and decided that he'd rented to a couple of bums.

After the Debate

'DID YOU GET A CHANCE to watch the cantadates?'

I turn at the slurred, loud challenge. Howard, the building super-intendent, is standing in the hallway, halfway between his basement apartment and the garbage room. He is wearing grey boxer shorts and a white sleeveless undershirt; his stockinged feet are planted well apart, but look steady enough. After five years, I should know it is impossible to stow my Glad bags without rousing him. Deaf as a post if you have a plumbing problem, he acquires radar when he has been drinking and needs an audience.

'I know you have your pillitical viewpoints,' he brays, though I'm sure neither of us could name one.

'Just a sec, Howard,' I stall, replacing the dented lid carefully.

'If you … er … have the opportunity.…'

I go silent after a few drinks. But alcohol grants Howard this weird emotional eloquence, even while it robs him of conventional sense. He sounds like a hick – *cantadate*, *pillitical* – but this also serves to make the subjects he's discussing seem ridiculous. Sly digs come naturally to him. *Did you get a chance.…* He saw Carol leave. What else would I be doing on a Wednesday night?

'If you're busy … occupied…' By the time I reach him, he has backed almost into his burrow, a roly-poly groundhog with the blood high in his face, offering me these excuses with a wounded bluster.

'I was just on my.…'

'C'mon, have a drink.'

'Thanks, Howard, but I'd better head back upstairs.'

To what? his pop-eyed expression might translate as.

'Have one.'

'Well, a small one, then.'

Howard installs me at the kitchen table with a glass with ice and about twice the rye I indicate. There is a dog calendar above the table, Dalmatians for May. Mrs Blakeney – all I've heard Howard, or anyone, call his wife – is sitting on the plush settee in the living room, smoking and watching 'The Nanny' on TV. Fran Drescher's big black hair and make-up might be a version, forty years gone, of Mrs Blakeney's own vertical wig or dye job, her powdered white face and poppy-red lipstick. She is grave-thin, all string and bones to Howard's lumps and folds. 'Give him ice, Howie, give him ice,' she said, by way of greeting, when I came in, shifting her profile to a neutral point between us and the television. Each time she sucks on her smoke, the cheek I can see becomes a wrinkled hollow, like an asshole. She has a drink going too. Her glass sits on the coffee table beside a porcelain poodle.

Six days ago, when Carol left with her last load – her new boyfriend popping his jaw muscles after I had declined to shake his hand – I watched the car go down the block, and then turned to go back inside and saw Mrs Blakeney's unnaturally coloured face in her basement window, watching me without expression from below the level of the lawn. Buried, I thought.

'Here's looking at you,' Howard says.

The rye comes over the ice, cool and harsh. Prickles in my stomach, then the warmth spreads. Normally I drink beer, which is not so dramatic. After three swallows, I'm as ready to discuss American presidential politics as anything else. Forget that last night Clinton and Dole were just two more advertisements I saw while dozing. I've been calling it quits early lately, getting into my pyjamas soon after dinner and settling back on the couch with my beer and the remote. It's been my pattern for a few months now; maybe longer, if you think of the years of drinking and watching a little less as leading up to it. The main difference, until a week ago, was that when I finally went to bed there was someone else asleep in it. At some point I had a hazy déjà vu of watching the Clinton-Bush debate, four years ago, with Carol. We were fairly new then, under a year, yet I could remember crawling in beside her, late, grateful for the warmth and her soft snoring.

'Thanks, Howard.'

Howard lights a cigarette. 'We should have those debates in Canada,' he says, dragging deeply. 'Make our politicians speak their minds.'

'We have had some,' I seem to remember.

'Not the same!' He blows out smoke and rye fumes.

It is better to nod than to have him explain. In five years here, I've learned that much.

'Clinton is a liar,' Howard asserts.

'I don't doubt it.'

'They call him Slick Willie, have you heard that?'

'Yes.'

'How can you elect somebody you can't trust to be president of the Yer-nited States? He may be smart but he flip-flops. That means he has no integrity.'

Maybe, I think; or it could mean he has a pulse. Integrity can be like coffin nails. And I've met people I could never begin to trust, even though I've never caught them in a lie. Most people, maybe.

But I say, 'Yes.'

Howard has a nose for faint agreement, though; it inflames him. He tops up both our glasses, and without asking, goes over to top his wife's. I hear her ice tinkle as he returns.

'Look at Dole,' he says. He puts up a stubby hand. 'I'm not saying he's perfect, maybe he's not as smart as your Rose Scholar. But watch him sometimes, the way he holds that crippled arm. This is a man who fought for his country. He's in pain every day.'

Sounds distracting, I think, swigging on the rye, which now packs a smooth wallop. I have a smart-ass interlude that I go through before I stop talking. But I don't forget Howard's own ramblings about destroyer duty in the North Atlantic, dolphins pretending to be torpedoes.

'That counts for something, all right,' I say.

Howard isn't fooled.

'No offence meant,' he leans in on a boozy cloud, 'but I think Clinton may be just a little too young for the job. That's why he has to tell so many whoppers. It's like a kid brother out with the big boys.'

'Well, I'll tell you what guys his age' – which is mine, roughly – 'talk about at work. We talk about retirement.'

Howard brings that hand up: warning, apology, fact. 'I don't mean anything by this now, don't take it wrong, but how many

nuclear bombs do you have your finger on at the steel company?'
I laugh; Howard doesn't.

'You wanna know how many lies Clinton's told? Clinton doesn't
even remember. Ever-body says Jer – Ginny – his girlfriend, the
Flowers girl, but that's just the start of it. Hell, I don't even care if a
man likes women.'
    Neither do I, but when Howard is in lecture mode he hates to be
agreed with; it distracts and angers him to be addressed at all. This is
the most comfortable phase of his rambling, for both of us. All he
asks is that my eyes and ears be turned his way, while my mind can do
what it likes. In a smoky darkroom I can develop my own pictures,
which the rye bathes in warm, syrupy amber.
    'Bob Dole has too much pride to attack him personally. But here
are some of the lies he said he's told the people...'
    One day, I went down to the lobby, where Carol was waiting for
her father to pick her up. They were going to go out to dinner
together. I remembered something I had to tell her and went down
after her. At the bottom of the stairs, I looked through a glass door
and saw Carol standing beside the outside door, smoking. It shocked
me. As far as I knew, she'd quit six months ago. Just the other day
we'd gone out for pizza to celebrate. She looked so utterly con-
tented, the smoke wreathing about her head, bringing her hand up
leisurely, that I thought of turning around and going back upstairs.
But there was something I had to tell her that couldn't wait. I've forgotten it now. She was embarrassed, of course. When I opened the
door, she dropped her hand quickly, as if to hide the evidence, and
got a sheepish look in her eyes, like a kid caught with her hand in the
candy jar. I wasn't mad, though I had to convince her of that. They're
her lungs. And I've never made the assumption that someone would
never, ever, lie to me; I think that's silly. What I was really feeling was
a kind of awe, and admiration, that she could fool me so completely,
keeping a part of her life that I knew nothing about.
    'I didn't want to let you down,' she said later, after she came back
from her dinner. And we laughed about all the subterfuge, the close
calls she'd had. 'You didn't guess? You never suspected?' she kept saying, as she told me about blowing smoke out the bathroom window,

burning incense, going for sudden walks. 'How could you not know?' she said, and then her eyes got shiny and she hugged me, saying, 'I love you.'

It was funny, because two years later, when I finally put two and two together about her seeing this other guy, the one she's living with now, she asked me the same question. *How could you not know?* We'd both been crying, and she looked up with a Kleenex held under her nose, and asked me that: 'How could you not know?' Apparently, it had been going on for a while, and it was a sheer fluke that I found out at all, spotting them in a car when I was driving the other way. And now I was the one who felt I had let *her* down, by not having any idea.

'I've gotta go,' I tell Howard. I drink what is left in my glass and set it down. But I don't go. I sit there. Howard has the stunned look he always gets when the end comes. Smoke seeps out of his nose and mouth. He blinks slowly.

'Have you heard from your wife?' Mrs Blakeney asks from the living room. Looking past Howard, I see her cheek suck in and relax. Another sitcom, a new one, has started up. She sets her empty glass down beside the poodle.

'We weren't married,' I say.

Mrs Blakeney turns her profile slightly more towards the TV. 'Oh,' she says, surprised. 'That's what you put on your application.'

'I know,' I say. Too tired to lie or explain, too worn out to do anything except relay the bald facts.

'You can be evicted for falsifying your application,' Mrs Blakeney says.

'So evict me.'

She brings her face far enough back around to let me know she wouldn't mind.

'I'm not the landlord,' she says with a thin smile.

'Tell him then.' I still have my hand around my glass.

'C'mon, now, that's enough of that,' Howard blusters, finding his voice finally. 'Mrs Blakeney's just kidding you. Aren't you, Dot?'

Dot. She doesn't answer.

Finally, then, I get to my feet. I feel like lead. Howard sees me to the door. Throwing a glance back toward the living room, he salutes me smartly, fingertips to temple and away.

'Commander-in-Chief,' he winks. 'Give 'em hell.'

'Harry Truman,' I say.

'Bombs away. The buck stops here.'

I shake Howard's hand, it feels soft and warm in my own, and leave.

Upstairs, in my own apartment, I walk around the rooms, stirred up somehow but not knowing what to do about it. I walk into the kitchen and stare at the dirty dishes and pizza and KFC cartons. I open the fridge and get a beer; it tastes weak after Howard's rye. I stand beside the couch, looking at the jumble of blankets and pillows and magazines. I walk into the bathroom and peer into the toilet and the bathtub, at the stuff around the sink. Then I walk into the bedroom and take in all the crap lying around there. Clothes, newspapers, cassette tapes. Nothing I see looks like it belongs to me. Some of it is Carol's, of course, but my own stuff doesn't seem any more my own than hers does. I don't live here.

Once you realize that, of course, the next step becomes obvious: Leave. Go some place else. Pack up and be gone by next weekend, when Carol comes back for the rest of her things. Let the Blakeneys show her to her boxes in the storeroom. But as good as that sounds I know I can't move that fast. First off, I have to decide where I'm going. Sipping my beer, I consider it. Some place you'd rather be than this. How could you not know?

The Stand-In

IT WAS 1980. Almost twenty years ago, now. Ganz was living on an Indian reserve, a small fly-in community hundreds of miles north of Sioux Lookout. He was there as the guest of his friend, a weatherman working for Environment Canada. After Ganz quit his job in Oakville, just getting tired of it, he wrote this weatherman, an old school friend, who invited him up for a visit. The weatherman was feeling bored, put-upon in some way that Ganz never quite understood, although they talked for days over glasses of smuggled-in rye. From what Ganz could see, he had an easy, do-nothing job; but, like many people in that position, he felt he should be doing even less. He told Ganz he could stay for the winter, helping him in return for room and board. Ganz had no other plans.

Soon Ganz was taking all of the weatherman's simple readings: temperature, barometric pressure, humidity, precipitation, wind direction and velocity. The weatherman napped most of the day. Incredibly, he complained about having to answer the phone when his supervisor called twice a week. Ganz wondered if his friend was losing his mind.

The situation worsened when the weatherman got involved with a local girl, a teenager named Crystal. This romance seemed to make the idea of any duties intolerable to him. All he wanted to do was go snowmobiling with her, speeding forty miles to the next village, where her brother had an empty cabin he let them use. Coming back for the supervisor's calls made his face go grey with hate.

Then, one day, he was all smiles. Forget about the supervisor, he told Ganz. From now on he would only call once a week; when he did, Ganz could tell him what he needed to know. Ganz assumed that money had changed hands.

Fuck him, the weatherman blustered, damning the supervisor but glaring at Ganz. The government was going to automate everything soon anyway. Why wait for them to lay him off?

Ganz paid no attention to these rationalizations. He realized that he and the weatherman were no longer friends, something he had begun to suspect. Yet here he was, *becoming* the weatherman in a sense.

The weatherman took Ganz to the Bay and bought him a parka and thick high boots and gauntlets. Ganz hadn't packed for the North. He signed a form allowing Ganz to ring up groceries on his Bay tab. Then he roared off on his snowmobile.

It was November 29. Minus 22 degrees Celsius, as Ganz recorded. The mildest day in a while.

'What you do with that stuff?'

Ganz looked up from the precipitation tray to see Andrew Mequanawap, his nearest neighbour. Andrew was a quick-stepping older man – maybe fifty, by his limber movements, but with a heavily lined brown face and almost no teeth. He had an oblique way of speaking, his words seeming to point to many things at once.

'My readings, you mean?' Ganz replied.

'All this shit.' Andrew's gloved wave took in all of the instruments and gauges littering the small yard like toys. His head, black-haired without a strand of grey, was bare to the minus-34-degree air, plus a wind-chill Ganz hadn't calculated yet.

'Nothing, Andrew. Just keeping track.'

Andrew liked to banter. But this time his face stayed stern. 'You warn me if it's going to snow? Some big storm or something?'

'Sure.'

'Bullshit.' Now he smiled, a black crease between two brown pegs. 'You're a government man.'

This he had said before. All the white men – teachers, policemen, the fly-in dentist who yanked teeth – were *government*.

Ganz mentioned the weatherman.

'He's gone. Disappeared.' Ganz must have looked dismayed, because Andrew added softly, like a doctor repeating his diagnosis, 'You're a government man, Fred.'

Then he walked away, his long strides crunching the snow. Ganz wanted to call after him, invite him in for tea, but the one time he had done so, Andrew had acted strangely, slurping the tea beside the kitchen door and leaving without a word.

The next morning, Ganz found a pickerel lying on his doorstep. A frozen, dull gold bar, dusted with snow, that he thawed on his kitchen table and fried, with potatoes and onions, for supper.

Andrew stopped by most days for a brief exchange. *Making his rounds,* Ganz thought, uneasy but also comforted. It was his only social life. He felt the strangeness of his position: not a local, not a government employee (officially); yet not just a visitor, either. Probably no one cared – you got by however you could in the north – but his situation weighed on him. It was a limbo. The native people he passed, on his walks or at the Bay, smiled in greeting, but he sensed an impenetrable mildness, a willed tolerance, in their courtesy.

Once before the teachers flew out for Christmas, Ganz got together with them and the policeman and his wife. Pouring illegal rum behind closed curtains in the teacherage, they bitched about the cold, the Bay prices, the sullen locals. The teachers seemed especially harried; one of them wouldn't return after the break.

Ganz told them about Andrew's *government* line. Someone joked about this being a *cabinet meeting.* They all got very drunk, cursing and laughing until the tears came. At the time it felt cathartic, though no one had suggested repeating it.

Ganz didn't hear from the weatherman. He didn't dare ask about him. Stints on UI back in Oakville had sharpened his sense of when to lie low, when to keep the facts of his life as unremarked as possible. Apparently, his credit was still good at the Bay, for Ganz's groceries kept clicking through. He had only a little cash, but there was nothing he needed. Environment Canada's cabin was snug, with a TV and VCR and stacks of movies. Sometimes, looking around at the bland, Ikea-style furniture, Ganz had the thought that he was in a deserted hotel. Like a science fiction movie. The power on, the kitchen well stocked, but all the other guests gone. *World of One.*

He slept fitfully at night, and napped often during the short, crystalline days. He felt like a mole huddled in a tunnel of cold. The snow machines would roar by, close, sounding like freight trains. Then silence again, like a stopped breath. He always set the alarm when he slept, since his readings had to be taken at four-hour intervals precisely. This irritated him, and he understood better the weatherman's gripes. The constrictions on him were loose, but constant; a fine mesh of duties and deadlines.

The supervisor still called, but less often. Sometimes he was clearly drunk, slurring fulminations about the coming automation that would 'fuck us all. Well, fuck *them!*'

At least once a week, Ganz checked his return air ticket in the drawer of the bedside table. Needing to know it was still there, still good. What kept him from shipping out immediately was partly masculine pride – he was twenty-seven – but mostly curiosity. He knew what was waiting for him back in Oakville: a job search. Then a job or welfare. This at least felt new.

The day after Andrew left the pickerel, Ganz walked down the shore to thank him.

Andrew was splitting wood, the axe blows cracking like gunshots. His shack always had a thick plume of smoke rising from it and split wood surrounded it in a thick, ragged wall. Firewood was scarce around the village; Andrew hauled it back from across the lake. Two mongrel dogs guarded the wood against the less industrious.

These dogs ran yapping at Ganz as he approached. Just before they reached him, their chains ran out, snapping them off the ground with strangled yelps.

'Thanks for the fish,' he called above the frenzied barking.

Andrew peered at him, shielding his eyes with his hand against the glare of sun on snow. His axe blade rested on the chopping block. He wasn't wearing a coat or gloves.

'You know what I thought of when I saw it,' Ganz heard himself babbling. 'Luca Brasi. You remember that scene in *The Godfather* when the Corleone family gets a fish wrapped in newspaper. "Luca Brasi sleeps with the fish." That's the first thing I thought of.'

Andrew was looking at him. He barked something in Ojibway at the dogs, which slunk back to the wood pile.

'You're bushed, Fred,' Andrew said.

Bushed. That word had come up often at the Christmas cabinet meeting. It meant teachers airlifted out, hysterical laughter, singing at the northern lights.

'No,' Ganz yelled, then realized it was silent now.

'You're bushed,' Andrew repeated, turning back to his work.

Walking home, Ganz had a sudden fearful suspicion of how Andrew's pronouncements could seem so malicious, mocking, comforting, goofy and profound – all of these things, at once.

Maybe they were just the truth.

What mainly got him through that winter was helping Andrew with his fish net. Andrew went out on the frozen lake once or twice a week. 'When I go,' he said, when Ganz asked him about his schedule.

One day in January, he pulled up on the snowmobile while Ganz was fiddling in the yard, adjusting the anemometer. 'Get on,' he yelled over the idling engine.

'Where we going?' said Ganz.

'Fishing.'

He got on behind Andrew. Putting his gauntleted hands up by Andrew's sides as they started, embarrassed to hold the other man any tighter. 'Hang on,' Andrew shouted as they left the island trail and bumped down onto the lake ice. Ganz hugged him, smelling his smoky campfire smell.

They flew across the frozen lake on a trail packed hard as tarmac by other snow machines. A runnerless metal sled, like an ambulance litter with curved sides, rattled along behind them. Strapped down on it was a tarpaulin-wrapped bundle. All around them was a sunshot plain of white, flowing in gentle waves and mounds, the soft brush line of the distant shore further blurred by Ganz's tearing eyes. The vastness of the winter was exhilarating. It seemed unimaginable that so much ice and snow could dissolve into blue waves by summer.

An empty oil drum marked the spot where Andrew fished. Two thick peeled sticks, like flagpoles, stuck out of the ice about thirty feet apart. Standing to one side while Andrew undid the straps on the sled, Ganz stared into the dense brush of the nearby shore. Another small island stood off in the distance. Light crashed all around, in eerie silence. Ganz had fished a few times in his life, sitting in a boat with a rod and reel, but he saw this was nothing like that. Anything might swim into a net under the ice.

Andrew had brought kindling and split logs under the tarp. He tossed these into the barrel and got a fire going. More than comfort, Ganz thought: life insurance. Andrew took a long-handled ice chisel from the sled and started digging with short thrusts around the marker stick nearest shore. Ice chips flew up. Ganz looked in the sled for another chisel to help, but there was only a coil of yellow nylon rope and Andrew's axe.

After a few minutes, Andrew paused, panting. Ganz by this time was so used to Andrew's stoical prowess, that his laboured breaths, his hands trembling from exertion, surprised him slightly. Andrew allowed him to take the chisel.

Ganz was clumsy at first. The chisel blade struck glancingly, or stuck upright. But he soon learned to aim the blade at the jagged edge of the hole, shearing off corners; to use, as Andrew had, short jabs. It was warmer, working. And he was young and strong; it made him feel proud that he dug the hole faster than Andrew. It was gratifying to strike the blow that brought dark water, like oil, bubbling through the slush.

But harder to finish the hole through the water, the chisel head slow and dreamlike.

When he looked up Andrew was watching him.

'Take your hood down. It's too hot.' It was minus 19 Celsius, a mild day by Ganz's changing standards.

'Get a tan?' Ganz said happily. Andrew shrugged.

Ganz took the chisel to the other marker, his job now, while Andrew tied the yellow rope to the net attached to the first pole. The system, once Ganz understood it, was ingeniously simple. After Ganz dug another, smaller hole, Andrew brought the rope down and tied it to the net on the second pole. He worked with bare hands in the frigid water. Then he untied the net from the pole, as he had done at the other end. Now they could haul the net down to the first hole without losing it; the continuous loop of net and rope was like a clothesline between two pulleys.

'How did you set it up the first time?' he asked.

'Bunch of holes,' Andrew muttered, securing his knots. 'Pass it along.'

Ganz tried to picture it, the work involved.

'It's easy. The ice is thin then.'

Down at the main hole, Andrew began hauling up the net. The yellow rope disappeared into the far hole. Ganz took off his gauntlets to help, but Andrew shook his head. 'You'll freeze,' he said. Embarrassed, Ganz tugged the gloves up again.

The first few yards brought empty net. Andrew, working quickly, dropped the wet mesh in folds beside the hole. Then, thrillingly, the fish came. First, a large spotted pike. Andrew disengaged its gills from the net and tossed it thrashing onto the ice. It flared its gills and lay still. Other fish followed: pale whitefish, glittering pickerel; something murky and large, with whiskers.

'What's that?' Ganz asked.

'Sturgeon. White men don't eat them,' Andrew said, gripping the greyish back. 'Just the eggs.'

All of the fish were alive, some barely, and Ganz wondered how long they had been struggling, swimming in place in the dark.

Two pike close together had snarled the net. Andrew's hands flew like a seamstress's as he untangled them.

'I caught a ten-pound pike once,' Ganz said. 'My girlfriend's mother made chowder out of it.'

'Too bony,' Andrew said dismissively, flipping the pike onto the pile of other fish. 'I keep them for my sentinels.'

His dogs. Sometimes Andrew used words that amazed Ganz. He had only been to grade eight, but he had a curious mind and he read the Bay manager's *Time* magazines after he'd finished them. He had described details of Ronald Reagan's inauguration to Ganz. 'He'll be good. Good for business,' Andrew announced, with an ambiguous sparkle in his eye. When Ganz ventured that he preferred Carter, Andrew retorted, 'No good for business.'

When the net was cleared of fish, Andrew motioned Ganz to begin pulling the yellow rope while he fed the net back into the hole. Hurrying now, Andrew tied the net back on to the pole, untied the rope, and jogged over to the other hole to do the same. Ganz felt a strange relief when Andrew stuck his hands out over the oil drum fire and rubbed them hard, his leathery face untensing with the warmth.

They packed the tools back on the sled, piling the frozen fish where the wood had been, and secured it all under the tarp and straps. Riding back behind Andrew, Ganz surrendered himself to a vision of remaining in the north, making his way up here. Surviving, as Andrew did, by his wits and muscle. Fishing. Shooting the occasional gift of a moose. Picking up summer dollars when the government needed a work crew to build new houses or clear brush. He knew it was a fantasy, but unlike the fantasy he was living, it made his life seem purposeful, vivid.

Back at Andrew's, standing safely out of range, he watched as Andrew used his axe to chop the pike up into chunks. The sentinels fell on the pieces he threw, gulping down the first frozen bites, then licking a piece into softness before swallowing it.

'When are you going again?' Ganz called hopefully.

'When I get hungry.' Andrew disappeared into his shack.

But Ganz went with him most times after that. Occasionally Andrew buzzed straight past in his snowmobile, moody or else asserting his autonomy. Or doing neither of those: he was a mystery to Ganz. Another mystery, which hurt Ganz at first, was that Andrew never offered him any fish to take home, even though Ganz was able to help more each time, and they were netting plenty of fish. The pickerel on the doorstep stood out as a lonely blessing. At some point, Ganz figured, he and Andrew had entered a zone where such simple trades, or gifts, were no longer possible. Why, he wasn't sure.

Once, he forgot himself with the older man, and it was like accidentally turning on the lights in a candlelit room.

It was a glittering February day. The sun actually felt warm again, like a hand on the back of his neck. Walking back from the Bay with his groceries, he took the long way round to pass Andrew's shack. Andrew was smoking by a pile of fresh-split, gleaming wood. For once, the sentinels, two puddles of dozing fur, stayed quiet.

'Hi, chief,' Ganz called. It was a simple, dumb mistake. He didn't mean anything by it. *Chief* had just come to mind – like guy, fella, buddy.

'Hello, Custer,' Andrew said without missing a beat. He actually brandished his axe, like a huge tomahawk.

Mortified, Ganz tramped on as though he had never meant to

stop. He passed through the yard of weather instruments, put away his cans and lay down for one of his long twilight naps, videos twittering in the background.

Two days later, they took in their best haul ever from the net. Two dozen fish, almost all of them whitefish and pickerel.

As the days lengthened toward spring, Ganz felt himself waking up. His eyes dilated with the light, swimming in new details. Sights jolted him: a bare-armed girl suddenly roaring out of cedars on a snowmobile at dusk, black hair streaming out behind her, nipples thrust against her T-shirt. It was one of the craziest, most sheerly beautiful things Ganz had ever seen, and he gaped after her, slack-jawed within his parka hood.

With Andrew's help, he put more names to the faces he greeted on his walks. Maggie, Crystal's aunt. Archie and, two steps behind him, toothless old Linda – his wife, not his mother. Young Benjamin hunting jays with his air rifle.

He even started studying the weatherman's textbooks and manuals, curious about the science he'd been bluffing at.

Stratus means 'layered'. Fog is a stratus cloud.

He felt like a tourist again. Displaced, curious; alive. Alive. To be home, he thought, is to be blurred, half-asleep; curled in your burrow. Like the kids – glue-sniffers, Andrew said – who scuffed along the boardwalk, or kicked the front step of the Bay in a mindless rhythm. Old people milling around the post office window at cheque time, or sitting motionless on their doorsteps. Now that he was emerging from it, the memory of his own numbness, matching the general malaise, chilled him.

Andrew had escaped the sadness, but Ganz thought that he would escape it anywhere. 'My son lives in Thunder Bay with his mother,' he said once, and something in his placid, unresentful tone told Ganz that Andrew would be exactly the same man wherever he found himself.

He no longer checked his airline ticket, sure now that he would use it soon. He thought that he would stay until break-up. See the ice melt into blue waves, then leave that new lake.

* * *

April began with a ten-day thaw. The temperature climbed to a balmy eight degrees in the midday sun, turning the road into muddy slush. Clouds of preposterous flies hovered over snowbanks. Snowmobile engines raced in the sticky snow, throwing up spray. The sound of dripping water was everywhere.

'Break-up soon?' he said to Andrew.

'No, Fred,' Andrew replied. 'Getting bushed?'

Ganz felt heartened that it was a question again.

They couldn't go out to the net. Pools of sinister grey were dotting the lake, seeping circles in the snow. The slush was too hard on the snowmobile, Andrew said, though he scoffed at Ganz's suggestion that they might go through.

'You dug those holes, Fred,' he reminded him.

Ganz thought of the fish, suspended below the roof of ice, fighting and resting, fighting and resting. How long before they gave up, or died of exhaustion?

One day, after taking his morning measurements, he stood by the front window of the Environment Canada cabin, sipping a Sanka. He felt happy, an awareness that had been sneaking up on him lately; the feeling usually coming with, part of, a mild anxiety about what he should do next.

Down the road, then, came a strange sight.

Three Indian women, bundled up, coloured scarves on their heads, were shuffling slowly between the half-frozen ruts. The two outside women supported the woman in the middle, holding her under the arms. Ganz heard a low moaning sound, like wind through a crack. As they drew near, he thought he recognized Maggie, Crystal's aunt, as the woman in distress. The moaning sound came from her lowered head.

He pulled back behind the curtain out of respect, or fear.

Something had happened. Was happening.

Ten minutes later, he was drinking another coffee, more acid for his prickling stomach, when the phone rang.

It was the almost forgotten supervisor. Drunk at eight in the morning, his voice shrill.

'The dishdric hea ...' he blurted, then the line went dead. Ganz knew, with an uncanny certainty, that the district head had just walked into the room. And, furthermore, that he would soon be flying up. It was as if he were in a dream tunnel, seeing events just before they happened, their causes dissolving behind him.

He put on his boots and wandered outside, just as Andrew pulled up on his snowmobile. He left the engine running.

Andrew's face was solemn, somehow strange. Like a dark leather mask hanging in shadow.

'Crystal went through the ice,' he said.

Ganz knew he meant Crystal *and* the weatherman.

'Are they … ? Did anyone … ?'

'They broke through,' Andrew said sharply.

'But you said…'

'It's a river over there. Currents.'

The fool. The damn fool, Ganz thought, close to tears.

Andrew throttled down. He stared down at his tough brown hands, as if searching for a softness that certain extreme situations called for.

'It's time, Fred,' he said gently. Ganz knew what he meant. 'I'll be back in an hour.'

He gunned the engine and veered away.

Ganz went back inside, dazed but strangely clear-headed. When he phoned the airport, the man who sold the tickets said, 'Eleven-thirty,' and hung up. Ganz felt giddy with tension. The gruff message was like the code word in a spy movie, the next link in the network that would smuggle him past Checkpoint Charlie.

He packed his bag quickly. Checking the rooms, he saw no evidence of his five-month stay but his breakfast dishes. He washed them and put them away.

Bouncing behind Andrew on the mangled road that led through bush to the airport, he felt the lake receding behind him. He would never see it blue. Behind him, the sled shimmied in the ice and mud, his pack strapped over the tarp like a midget's body bag. At the airport, Andrew and the ticket agent muttered together in Ojibway. Standing to one side in the stuffy shack, Ganz felt a deep shame, partly bracing, for causes obscure to him. It wasn't the deception he had participated in, which seemed minor, almost humdrum, one more loop in a vast web of scams. What made his shoulders slump was the dim sense of a larger sin, something pervasive that had snagged him. Carelessness, perhaps; or its twin, ignorance.

He thought he saw embarrassment flicker, for the first and only time, in Andrew's eyes as they shook hands goodbye.

'Hope you get a cold snap,' Ganz said. Or a thaw, he thought.

'Why, Fred?' Andrew asked.

'To get the fish.'

Andrew gave his thin smile, which now seemed less ironic, more clearly bitter. 'They're not going anywhere.'

Sitting in the Twin Otter with the other passengers, Ganz watched the pilot and the ticket agent toss the freight up to the co-pilot, who stacked it behind webbing attached to either wall. He imagined the fish, wriggling more faintly. Down the road, two boys sprang from the bushes and jumped on Andrew's sled. Ganz watched through the plane's little window as they rocked the sled from side to side for a little ways, then tumbled off again. Andrew never looked back or slowed.

In Toronto, where he drifted a few months later, Ganz got a job driving cab for an old man who owned three cars. The old man's son, also the dispatcher, told Ganz that he could safely keep 15 per cent of his fares undeclared; his father would overlook that much.

Ganz wondered briefly when his face had become the kind of face you knew would understand, and need, that kind of information.

The Train

EVERYTHING WAS GOING FINE, we were almost there, until she said, 'Hold on,' and reached over the side of her bed. I could hear her rummaging in the bedside table, and then she came up again with something long and floppy. I looked at it, and then I sat up and turned on the light.

'I'm sorry,' I said. 'Call me square.'

Neither of us said anything for a few minutes after that. She plumped up her pillow and sat like I was, with her back to the wall, staring straight ahead. Like passengers on a bus or train. I hadn't met her eyes since she came up with the rubber tubing. Out of the corner of my eye I could see it lying between us, brown and hollow at both ends, like a snake with its head and tail lopped off. After a bit, she picked it up, holding it in her thumb and forefinger, and dropped it over the side of the bed with a plop. Silence. I was working up a fantasy of a snake slithering up the bedclothes towards some moans and movement, unaware of the twin machetes that awaited it, when she said:

'It's because I don't come, isn't it?'

'No,' I said.

She adjusted the pillow behind her back. 'If it's Ryan, I told you how sick he is. He's out of the hospital now, but he'll be staying with his parents for weeks, maybe months.' We snuck a quick look at each other, the train clear of the city and entering into the rhythm of farmland.

'Windsor isn't exactly around the corner,' she said.

'I know.' I knew everything, except why permission seemed to yawn like a lazy ogre.

'Then what?' Her irritation showed itself suddenly. 'Tell me. I'm the one who got snubbed.'

'I'm sorry. It's not you. It's me.'

'Look at me.'

Her eyes were a milky brown, wide and slow-blinking. They

63

looked like my son's eyes before they darkened. I turned off the lamp, and the room shrank back down to a bed and bed only. No pictures, no dressers and closets. No antique cherrywood chair that no one sat in, positioned in front of a window.

'Thank you.'

Somehow, we got back to where we'd been. There was no effort, no carryover. A snake had attacked, we had disposed of it.

'You know what I think,' she said, afterwards.

'What?'

'I think Mr Sceptic is really Mr Psychic.'

'What do you mean?' We were lying on our backs, touching at shoulder and hip. Now the train had changed direction fantastically and was heading straight up through the ceiling towards the stars.

'You got scared.'

'I admit it.'

'You knew I wanted to tie you up.'

'Me?' I said, so surprised that it sounded like a joke.

Hymen's Fool

'YOU'VE GOT SUCH A MOUTH!' Nancy told Ina, soon after they started working together in Medical Records. It was the day the X-ray Casanova came into Emerg dangling a splinter from his side, harpooned by a snow fence while skiing. 'Open season on sperm whales?' Ina cracked, without raising her head from her file. Nancy slid a hand over her giggles, her dark eyes dancing. 'What a mouth!' she said again, sounding awed.

They called it 'the Mouth' – this organ that gave vent to accurate spite, to malicious mirth.

Two years later, Nancy asked Ina to be the maid of honour at her wedding. 'You're like my big sister,' she said, her eyes filling, at Zoos where she had taken Ina for lunch. Am I? Ina wondered, while keeping big-sisterly track of two men at the bar who had been eyeing Nancy.

She and Nancy rarely socialized outside of work, though they gabbed all day at their desks, and at lunch in the hospital cafeteria. Mostly, they talked about Nancy's life: her problems with her mom, her future dreams of MKC: Marriage, Kids, Career. Ina was better at sorting out the problems than at sharing the dreams. Nestled in luscious dark curls, Nancy's heart-shaped face looked unnervingly like a valentine; watching her small white teeth as she talked or laughed, Ina felt pangs under her breastbone. What would the world give those milk teeth to gnaw on?

'I'd be thrilled to!' she heard herself gush.

The answer seemed to rush out on its own. Over another pitcher of draft, she made Nancy laugh with horror stories of married life, which Ina, though unmarried, was assumed to have a better window on. It felt like the first of many for-old-times'-sake drinkups. Meanwhile she kept an eye on the two at the bar. Nancy was the only child of parents who had separated when she was young. She was anxious to marry, to establish what her parents had let slip away. She credited Ina with showing her that Tony was the right man. But Ina, who had no strong opinion of Nancy's fiancé except that he was good-looking and shrugged too often, had merely helped Nancy see that *she* felt that. The job coming up in Personnel – *that* was what she had advised her to go after. Nancy had hesitated; Ina had seniority, and Personnel, where one worked with the public, was considered a better department. 'But I like diseases,' Ina said, spreading her arms to the file cabinets around her. Really, she knew, she was just too stuck. At forty, you needed a heavy goad to move. Sticks at your back.

After Nancy left the bar to meet Tony, with a hug and a murmured, 'Thank you. This is starting right,' Ina stayed by herself for a while, drinking coffee. The two men left and, except for the bartender, she was alone. As the coffee took hold against the draft, her doubts returned. *Made a fawner*.

Suddenly, glancing at her watch, she realized that she was late for picking up Mick.

Outside the warehouse on Spring Street that Fossil Fuel rented for practice, the band was huddled with their instruments in the nippy fall air. Mick reminded her with a grimace of his bad back – aggravated by the oversized amp – and Ina backed the van as far up the narrow alley as she could.

'Hi, I!' the musicians called, loading their equipment in the back. They thought she was 'a good shit', according to Mick. Which meant, Ina knew, an affable roadie type rather than a Yoko Ono, with ideas of her own. Joking with them in the rear-view, she kept seeing her skin in close-up, dry, lined around the eyes, and framed by crinkly brown hair; behind her, the sweaty, young, longhaired faces. Mick, though he was a few years younger than Ina, was balding, in patches rather than fashionably. Grumpily giving unnecessary directions – his blood sugar low before dinner, and disheartened after the rehearsal, where sonic reality trampled on the dream – he made a good father.

'Don't sell yourself short,' he said when she told him about Nancy. Beer, and the sandwich she had given him to tide him over, had made him generous. 'She probably knows she needs someone steady rather than some airhead.'

Ina remembered the time Nancy had come over after an

argument with Tony. Steadiness was not what Mick had seen in Nancy's stretch denims, his eyes rising with effort to her face in order to commiserate.

Sitting at the table while Ina made dinner, he took his guitar out of the case and changed the strings, then fiddled with an electronic tuner that had been acting up, trying new batteries. Getting the dream back. When the tuner worked finally, and he wound the E string up to pitch, he joked, 'This marriage talk scares me, though. Don't get any ideas.'

'I won't,' said Ina, deboning a chicken breast.

He had warned her he wasn't into marriage when they moved in together. Now, two years later, she felt the same way: not into it. They had met at the art gallery, where he picked up work building shipping crates and helping with installations. She had gone there in the hope of meeting someone. Then, his flyaway hair and twisted smile, both thinner now, had seemed exciting. In his grim jokes about the masses – 'zombies', 'clones' – she had found a tonic blackness; but, quite quickly, it had begun to seem more like a tantrum, partly suppressed. A kicking at the world, as at a rotten egg you can't break out of.

Behind her as she diced the vegetables, she heard the chords of 'Siege State', Fossil Fuel's current hope for a single.

When the wedding plans began in earnest, it was hard to escape the impression of being herded. Nancy had it laid out like Operation Overlord. There were conferences, consultations, lists and diagrams. 'Just the main events,' Nancy promised, a higher than usual note in her giggle, at the first briefing of the bridal party, over pizza at Valentino's. Ina and the bridesmaids, Jonquil and Rose, exchanged benign smiles, a compact of pleasantry that must last nine months, long enough to close on Berlin.

When the two girls had flounced in to join them, Ina had resisted the urge to crack, 'Well, so much for floral arrangements.' She had the Mouth tightly leashed. Besides, she wasn't sure she could say it lightly enough. The few times she had been out with the two, she had caught herself marvelling at the extent to which the girls did bloom as lushly as their names. Buds of breasts and bums on slender, stalk-like bodies; all pointing to the fragrant, petal-soft faces. Ina knew she had never been that radiant. Too *sturdy*, her dad's fond euphemism.

Florist, caterer, minister, DJ, hospitality director, photographer. Crucial people. Fittings, shower, rehearsal, rehearsal party, ceremony, reception, dinner and dance. Crucial events. Other variables: weather, Nancy's father (would he attend?), the performance of the groom's party.

Regarding the latter, Jonquil said, tugging cheese from behind a napkin, 'I think I can keep Kevin and Dirk in line.'

Sawing at her crust, Ina looked up quickly to catch the spirit this was said in. But Jonquil's pale eyes were not cold. She believed in Ina's matronly capabilities. Nancy had had a heart-to-heart with her oldest, sometimes fiery friend, explaining to her why she had chosen Ina to be at her side. 'She understands. She understands,' Nancy assured Ina, who wished she had got the explanation.

Finally, Nancy handed out typed sheets titled *Nancy and Tony*, a kind of flow chart culminating in the highlighted *June 12*, with stars beside each event at which the bridesmaids were needed. Ina was relieved to see that her sheet did not have many more stars than the other two. The atmosphere became sombre as the three, watched by Nancy, studied their sheets while sipping coffee. The generals, considering. Nancy broke the strained silence by asking, 'I know we'll forget a million things before it's over. But can anyone see one, right off?'

Ina took a chance. 'Party hats?' she suggested.

The table dissolved into giggles. 'Party hats!... Party hats!' Rose pretended to strap a little hat under her chin and balance it teeteringly. 'See?' Nancy said to the other two. 'See?' It *was* what they wanted from her, after all.

Ina began to go regularly to Nancy's house, to plan and to get to know Nancy's mother, Dot, a chubby agreeable woman, a few years Ina's senior. Ina and Dot exchanged knowing smiles about Nancy's exuberance and nerves. *Just wait*, these smiles seemed to say.

At the first fitting at the Olympia bridal shop, the three younger women, after their willowy figures had been measured, enjoyed watching the more problematic sizings of the older women.

'Lend me some, I?' Rose said, mock enviously, as the saleslady extended the tape measure around Ina's ample bust.

'She's in proportion,' the saleswoman corrected, with a glance at Ina's hips. Dot, a buxom ally, smiled sympathy.

When Nancy finally found the dress she would wear, Dot's eyes filled with tears. 'You look like a princess, dear,' she murmured. Nancy did. And though part of Ina found the whole ritual preposterous, trussing Nancy up in white like some tissue-wrapped door prize, tears started in her own eyes at Dot's heartfelt exclamation. After that, the bridesmaids' selections were a distinct comedown, which Ina figured was only right. Voile in dusty pink, with ruffles at the neck and wrist. Ghastly.

'How goes the farce?' Mick asked at home. He had a pot of chili started. Rehearsal must have gone well. Ina kissed him on the cheek and took over.

When she got the Personnel job, Nancy marched up to Ina's desk and announced grimly: 'They're going to split us up.'

Ina, putting envy on hold, had to convince her that she had a reason, and a right, to be glad. It reminded her of breakups with vacillating boyfriends, where you had to show them how to forget you.

There came a point when you had to get tough.

'I should never have applied,' Nancy was mumbling at her desk, worrying a tendril of hair with her forefinger.

'Now, look!' Ina growled and swivelled in her seat, the signal for Nancy to do the same. Hands on knees, they faced each other. 'You did apply. You should have. You got the job. That's great. Life goes on. Okay?'

'Okay.'

The Mouth finished up. 'Just promise me one thing.'

'What?'

'When Grayson starts telling you stories about his sick wife, you switch to pantsuits immediately.'

'Oooh!' Nancy pressed her bare knees together and shook her shoulders, the sparkle back in her brown eyes.

Perceptiveness, or a capacity for perceptiveness, flickered in those eyes, something firmly rooted that was waiting for her youth to pass before it could poke through. It brought back Ina's doubts about the wedding. What thread would connect them now? How could it prove strong enough, when even the first thread had been slim? Another possibility, that Nancy's choice had never been as capricious or sentimental as it seemed, that something more infallible than little-sister dependence had guided her all along, flashed through Ina's mind, trailing implications both vague and sinister. The bother about being miscast was easier to consider.

Promptly on the first of December, a Christmas card arrived at Ina and Mick's apartment. Ina opened it under Mick's mocking eye. Adoration of the Brat, he called the season. A slip of paper fell out, an invitation to a pot-luck dinner next Saturday. Ina checked her *Nancy and Tony* flow chart and found, next to Saturday's date, '(?) *Wedding Party Get-Together* – something intimate.'

'What, so we can all pretend we're friends on the big day?' sneered Mick. He was curled like a big foetus on the floor, his naked head near his knees, his hands limp. A new back exercise. The Peavey amp, made for teen jammers or established musicians with roadies, was killing him.

'You're not invited,' Ina informed him. 'Just the wedding party.'

'Good.' But he seemed to curl tighter.

When Ina confirmed with Nancy at their next lunch, Nancy asked her to bring a dessert, and added ominously, showing her little teeth as she got up from the table, 'Oh, and don't forget a sleeping bag and your PJs.'

'My p–,' Ina began, but Nancy was gone. Ina was left to dread what in all likelihood was shaping up to be a slumber party, something she had not attended in decades, while she tried to separate the gristle from the beef in her Irish stew.

At Jonquil's high-rise on Saturday, cut flowers were arranged in vases in the living room. Along with the lit tapers, they gave the room, with its wicker furniture and stacked black electronics, a sombre, ritual feel – like a Japanese funeral, Ina thought, without having any idea what that would be like. Cushions were arranged in twos around a glass coffee table. *Something intimate.* Dismayed, at first, to be paired with Nerf, alias Bob, Ina was relieved when the best man turned out to be a frizzy-haired, roly-poly little fellow, older than his years, who sold insurance and seemed willing to laugh at any joke, without inflicting many of his own. He was Tony's childhood friend, acquired before he had moved up to the flashier Kevin and Dirk.

Dinner was fun, actually. After Rose's shrimp dip and crackers, came Jonquil and Nancy's collaboration on shish kebabs and caesar salad – all delicious, and the skewers were fun, pieces dropping off them at humorous moments, Tony and Dirk jumping up to stage a mock duel with mini-swords. The men's contribution was the stack of beer in the hallway, which they took turns running to with empties and refills. Her trifle went over well, no one noticing Mick's gouge, which she had plugged with whipping cream.

After Spanish coffee, and a little speech on friendship by Nancy followed by teary hugs, the men were shooed out. They took most of the unused beer. Each of the men hugged each of the women at the door. Tony whispered in Ina's ear, 'Nancy's lucky.'

Stepping back to look at him, Ina, slightly tipsy, returned the compliment. 'Yes, she is.'

Tony shrugged, the case of beer lifting.

Then the part of the evening she had dreaded began. One by one, the girls went to the bathroom and came back dressed for bed. Nancy, Jonquil and Rose wore men's pyjamas which bagged becomingly on them – like Audrey Hepburn wearing Gregory Peck's in *Roman Holiday*. Wading from the bathroom in her beige nightgown, Ina felt walrus-y.

'Our chaperone!' yelled Jonquil, throwing her arm around Ina's shoulders. But Ina caught the sparks, as if thrown from her red hair, in Jonquil's pale green eyes.

Ina drank too much of the beer the boys had left. All of them did. This, Ina remembered, was part of it. Getting sloshed. So were the giggled stories about sex. Years before, they had been about first sexual experiences; now, they were about the last, or married sex. Alpha and Omega. These took the place of the horror stories told at camp by the last light of the campfire. The four of them were already in their sleeping bags on the living-room floor, the glass table pushed aside, only one candle still burning. Nancy was dozing off.

Jonquil told hers first. 'Dad told me, this was after he and Mom had been living apart about a year, that they hadn't had sex in six years. Can you imagine? I thought he might be just saying it, trying to make excuses for how shitty he'd been, but Mom said the same thing, later.'

Nancy, her eyes closed, said, 'That's one problem I *won't* be having with Tony.'

Ina, seeing the shrug and the good grip on the case of Blue, knew she was wrong.

'My mother told me this really weird story about her aunt's friend.' It was Rose, the quietest of the three, talking. She was propped up on an elbow. Ina propped herself up, too, to hear her better. She and Rose faced each other across the supine forms of Jonquil and Nancy. The candle played eerily over Rose's pale skin and button nose, her pageboy of blond hair, making Ina think of a dead squire, reanimated to tell of a rumoured battle.

'This woman, Mrs ... I can't remember her name, but after her husband died and was buried, she came to my aunt crying about something she had done. My mother thought it was really weird. So did my aunt, but Mrs – Whatever – was so upset that she told her it was understandable. Apparently, her husband had a heart attack and died in his sleep. She woke up and found him dead.'

'Oh, my God,' murmured Nancy.

'Yeah, but get this. Before she called the ambulance or whatever, she took his clothes off and took pictures of him lying there. With her camera.'

'That's gross,' said Jonquil, opening her eyes.

'That's what she was so upset about. But why she did was the strange part. Apparently, even though they'd been married thirty years or something, she'd never seen him. Not all of him, I mean. They'd had kids and everything.'

'How?' asked Nancy. She was awake now, too.

'I don't know. Through the pyjamas, I guess. I mean, how big a hole do you really need, right, I?'

Ina could only nod.

'Anyways, she said she couldn't put him into the ground without looking at him at least once. And then, I guess she figured once wasn't enough to have a very strong memory. So she took the pictures. Weird, huh?'

What removed Ina neatly from her companions, during the brief discussion that followed, was their astonishment. They reacted as if to a report of a Bigfoot sighting. Ina found the story very sad, but not freakish. Young people thought there were things that couldn't be held in, couldn't be suppressed. Part of growing older was a greater respect for people – for their power to turn away, even for a lifetime, from what they didn't want, or couldn't afford, to see. She was glad that Rose's story was considered the capstone to the evening and that she was not called on to provide one. She couldn't imagine a story she could tell that would properly appall her slumber mates, without at the same time depressing her.

Over the winter, Ina felt herself slipping away from the wedding. Without Nancy nearby (instead, a grey-haired temp prattling about 'hubby'), it was hard to keep pumped up. Mick's regular reminders that it was all a farce didn't help, or did help, in terms of speeding up an inevitable drift. One night, egged on by him, she phoned Nancy to suggest that it might be better, after all, if Jonquil was the maid of honour and she was a regular bridesmaid.

'I?' Nancy's voice, after listening to Ina's quick speech, was hushed.

'Yes?'

'I need to know one thing, I.' Ina said nothing in the pause. 'I need to know you're kidding. You are kidding, right?'

'Well, sort of,' Ina answered, her mind racing ahead of itself to improvise. 'I want to be your maid of honour,' she heard herself say. The blur in her peripheral vision was Mick turning away in disgust. 'It's just that ... well ...' The Mouth stumbled, unable to joke or tell the truth – 'it's been a rough time, lately.'

In the end, she blamed it partly on PMS, partly on winter blues, on boredom at work, and, in a whisper when Mick went to the bathroom, on troubles at home. Kicking herself even further down the hole, she implied that it could be the start of a mid-life crisis, something Nancy wouldn't know about yet.

But Nancy came through. 'Don't bet on it. I saw my mom go through some pretty rough times after Dad left.' Ina, miserable, had to allow herself to be consoled and advised. Nor was the advice, had it applied, unsound. In the end, she had to agree when Nancy said it was probably the best talk they had ever had.

'Partners?'

'Partners.'

'I knew I could count on you. That's why I picked you.'

As the wedding date approached, Nancy called sometimes late at night, relating breathlessly that she was so keyed up that even with her sedatives she was finding it hard to sleep. Ina hardly knew what to say to this. How to answer Nancy's high-pitched question: 'Isn't this unbelievable?' Yes, it was. She began letting the answering machine take the call when the phone rang after eleven p.m. But that seemed a worse betrayal, lying beside Mick while Nancy sang to them in the dark of her snags and successes.

'Let's hope she doesn't pull a Linda,' Mick remarked sardonically after one of these calls.

And he told a story about his cousin's wedding.

Ina wondered why she had not heard the story before. It was the sort of story Mick relished, an offering of absurdity to a bankrupt idol. She suspected that the answer was another woman, whoever he had been with at the wedding. Someone he had to leave out of the story, though he found it difficult to do so.

A shy, passive, eager-to-be-married Catholic girl, Linda had become hysterical at the altar – not decorous tears of joy, but piercing shrieks and wails lasting many long minutes, impervious to the priest's attempts to calm her, while the audience, sober to begin with because of doubts about the groom, watched in dry-eyed astonishment.

'We're not talking crying,' Mick emphasized. 'This was more like an exorcism.'

'Why didn't you tell me this before?' Ina asked.

Mick grinned. 'Didn't want to give you any ideas.'

'What, about screaming at your wedding?'

Mick, not a major appreciator of the Mouth, laughed this time.

A few days later, he brought home a book from the gallery library showing Rubens's copy of the Aldobrandini Wedding, an ancient Roman frieze-painting. He pointed out Hymen, smug in his laurel wreath. 'There he is, the little prick.'

That night they 'did the nasty' for the first time in a while. Mick had got the phrase from an interview with an English rock star. Ina found it funny, too, though she wondered sometimes just what it meant to him. Was he strapping her on, like a guitar? Plugging in? Power chording? In their case it was not so much nasty, which she thought might be interesting, as frantic; but nice, just the same. Warm, afterwards.

It seemed to be part of a more general rapprochement between them that winter. Fossil Fuel cut down their rehearsal schedule, meeting instead at a bar with their songbooks but no instruments. Discussing where they were headed, Ina gathered, though Mick did not talk to her about it. He did, however, finally pay his accumulated driving fines so that he could drive the van himself. She appreciated that, as well as other small, but long-awaited changes. He was still loath to cook, but he helped more often with the dishes, and sometimes phoned her from the art gallery to see if they needed anything at the IGA. Ina saw all this as part of a long-overdue process of taking stock, settling down. Settling, in general: for, with. Now that it was finally happening, she could be more generous about the forces that had delayed it. Mick knew he was stuck. He didn't have the talent, the luck, the money – the ticket. There was even a kind of nobility in his forlorn kicking against the pricks. She had seen that, once; now she glimpsed it again.

She had accommodated herself to seeing it through with Nancy. You paid, along with them, for friends who didn't know themselves. When, after one of Nancy's frantic midnight calls, her doubts flared up again, it was Mick who allayed them, saying with a shrug, 'She's a young chick. She's just trying to have her fairy tale.' Ina hugged him in gratitude. That was exactly the viewpoint she had been struggling to find. You didn't have to believe in the story to read it over someone's shoulder.

One day, late in May, she came home one day to smell her own stew recipe filling the kitchen. Something missing, she could tell, but she was too grateful to mention it. Mick opened two beers and asked her to sit down with him at the table.

'Ina.'

Ina felt a fluttering excitement in the pit of her stomach, like a vibrating seed pod about to extrude a stem. She realized, as Mick searched for words, that she had harboured this expectancy for a long time; it had never died; blocked, it was what sharpened the Mouth, gave it inexhaustible comebacks; it was also one with the light in Nancy's eyes, the pure darting hope, the chattering white teeth.

Fossil Fuel was going on the road.

They had managed to line up a few gigs, one-night stands, to get them as far as Seattle, where they were going to take their best shot. They thought they were ready. They would be gone as long as it took, or until they'd had enough. He hoped she wouldn't consider it the end of them, but he understood that she might. She didn't have to give him an answer right away. She should think about it. They were taking the van.

At the rehearsal, a week later, there were no embarrassing questions about Ina's date. Nancy had paved the way. With what they had already heard about Mick, nobody missed him, except perhaps to have their bad impression confirmed, a forgoable luxury.

At the church, Ina concentrated on her role and was good at marshalling others into their places. At Dot's house afterwards, she continued this efficient role: whisking plates away, refilling glasses. Service, done well, left little room for talk. Bob, bless him, though he had brought a date, was attentive. Nerf was a good name for him: soft, squeezable, safe for kids of all ages.

It was still uncertain if Nancy's father would attend the wedding, or if he had even received his invitation. He was 'hard to get hold of', Nancy said; Dot called him a drifter. When Mr Cavallin did appear at the reception party, a ripple of reaction widening his entrance, Ina was surprised at his appearance. He was a small, shrewd-looking man with thick glasses. He looked, not dissolute, but almost worse, like some kind of puzzled librarian. He drank a cup of coffee behind some people, then left.

Soon after, down on her knees behind the bar getting more mixer, Ina overheard, from close to her on the other side, 'The maid of honour is certainly pulling a long face.'

The phrase 'maid of honour', rather than her name, prevented her for a second or two from recognizing the familiar voice. It was Dot.

Someone whose loyalty, though limited in value, she had thought assured.

'It must be difficult for her. I think she's a good sport,' countered a stranger's voice.

Ina wondered hopelessly *which* circumstance she was being commended for battling with grace? She wanted to rise and confront them, shame them with her presence, but the thought of being exposed as an eavesdropper kept her on her knees. She had to remind herself that she was blameless as well as invisible. But there seemed a kind of guilt in invisibility. People couldn't make allowances for what they couldn't see.

She waited until new voices had approached the bar to rise, smiling, with her Coke and ginger ale.

It was shortly after that, some guests beginning to leave, that Ina noticed Nancy standing by herself in the corner, looking pale, her eyes wide and unfocused. With her new, polished view of things, Ina was not surprised. Eleventh-hour jitters were part of the rite. She finished filling her ice cube trays while keeping an eye on Nancy. When she hurried out of the room, Ina followed her.

She found her upstairs in the spare bedroom. Sobbing, her fists clenched at her waist.

Ina sat her down on the edge of the bed. She put her arm around her and waited for it to come out. Nancy had chosen well. When Rose peeked around the door frame, Ina twirled her free hand eloquently: *It'll be all right; keep others away.* She could hear her hovering outside the door.

It was the tension that did it. Turning yourself into a guided missile, coil by spring by hard metal casing, when every sign told you that the target wasn't worth hitting, wasn't worth aiming the whole arsenal at anyway. Nancy, sensible despite her fantasies, was bound to crack eventually. To her credit. Or was it seeing her father again? For some absurd reason, Ina thought that Mick, driving or tuning up somewhere, would be proud of her for these clear thoughts. Yes, she was *steady*.

When Nancy's sobs turned to sniffles, and then slowed, Ina handed her a Kleenex. None of this was hard. Only avoiding it, questioning it, was. 'Shh,' she said, stroking her shoulder. 'It's all right.'

'It's J-Jonquil,' Nancy stammered, then with a glance at the door, lowered her voice. 'It's Jonquil. She likes Tony. All night, she's been flirting with him. The night before my wedding.'

'Shh, shh,' Ina said, quelling a fresh flood of tears. 'It's nothing.'

The next morning, dressing herself after her bath, she imagined the other people who would be at the wedding doing the same thing. Across the city, all the guests and participants, sitting in baths, seeing pieces of themselves in mirrors, tugging fabric into position, cinching belts. Checking the final result, never what you hoped. She made herself a cup of tea and, getting milk from the fridge, saw her cellophane-wrapped bouquet, cooling. She sat down at the kitchen table. The apartment was roomier without the music equipment. It looked almost like it had when she moved in.

She kept monitoring herself for 'big day jitters'. Any woman had reason to feel them; that, at least, united them. But she was amazed by her own calm. Pleasantly heavy, almost sluggish, like a slow tide of efficiency pushing expected actions up a beach. Her fears had been groundless; there wasn't that much to this. She could be steady for Nancy.

The limo arrived to take her to Dot's house. Sitting on the plush seat, far behind the driver with his peaked cap, Ina imagined herself as a millionairess being transferred in seclusion from one setting to another, an air bubble in the pulse of common humanity. But the driver, sallow, middle-aged, came out of character to turn, grinning, and say, 'This is your chance. Leave 'em hanging and go for a joy ride.' He had seen the Mouth, or something.

Ina smiled coolly and looked out the tinted window. *A joy ride*.

Nancy was seated on the edge of a kitchen chair, her gown billowing around her. Wisps of dark hair, stark as ink marks missed by Whiteout, fringed her pale forehead beneath her tiara. Jonquil was giving her chamomile tea with honey and lemon, holding the cup for her and handing it to her when she asked for it. Nancy held herself very still so as not to crack the creation. Her arm rose slowly to the teacup and she retracted her lips to slide a little of the tea between her small teeth, inserting it into the mask of make-up and lipstick.

'We're lucky it's not too hot. Now if the rain will just hold off long enough,' Dot said, as Rose and Ina nodded gravely. 'And we get our bad actors sorted out,' she added in an undertone to Ina, when Rose took over with the teacup. Mr Cavallin was still a question mark.

Ina took responsibility for the dress, bunching it away from doors and corners, tucking pieces of it into the limo, the driver, solemn now, holding the door. She sat beside Nancy on the back seat, holding her hand. She could feel it trembling. Nancy stared at her mother and her friends, who stared back at her from the facing seat. Their faces were not so much rapt, as empty: exhausted by emotion, or conserving it for when it would be needed. A tension-easing crack was called for, but Ina couldn't think of a thing to say. She had banished the Mouth too thoroughly for it to be recalled on short notice.

Mr Cavallin had showed, was waiting at the church door. As Jonquil and Rose took Nancy's arms, Nancy glanced back at Ina, as if to say, 'You understand?' The scene in the room the night before had ended with a tearful reconciliation, the three girls hugging in a tight circle while Ina clucked approvingly, patting their arched backs. Now she smiled.

Following up the steps with Dot, it occurred to her that she had not seen, in a while, that wiser, becoming-perceptive look in Nancy's eyes. It was disappearing. Perhaps she had had it wrong, all along. There was no older person waiting to emerge, only one anxious to say goodbye, in this ritualized farewell. In that case, once again, Ina was the right person to see her off.

The slow walk up the aisle, amid the eyes, was only mildly trying; also mildly tickling to the vanity. It happened in too much of a blur to produce strong sensations. What did celebrities get from it?

Then she was at the altar. Dirk and Kevin, slab-like in black, beaming. Bob, thankfully, squat and already slightly rumpled. Tony suitably imposing, the straight black line of shoulder weighted down. Jonquil and Rose, a-bloom beside her.

They half faced the congregation, waiting too, one of the modern customs Nancy thought would freshen things up. Ina could see the groom's contingent – relaxing, since she did not know them – and, when she turned slightly, Nancy's relatives. Dot looked mildly confused; Ina focused on her.

The flower girl and ring-bearer, Nancy's cousins, like midgets with shining faces, tottered up the aisle accompanied by soft groans.

The Wedding March began.

Scanning the blurry faces below her, Ina thought of the missing one. Though he had never said he would come, dangling that decision (like so many others) over her head, she had expected in the end to catch Mick's mocking eye, his mouth twisted in derision, his bald spot trapping the light. She had amused herself wondering how she would meet that look when the time came. Would it make her smile? Frown? Could she ignore it, snubbing his snubbing? Nothing would scare him like a good shit turned clone.

As the Cavallins, father and daughter, drew near, Ina flushed to see that Mr Cavallin was watching her with his somehow penetrating myopia. When he came close enough, and was sure he had her eye, he winked. Behind a bubble of glass, his flesh closed and opened like an oyster shell. Ina looked away quickly.

Now Nancy was beside her, staring ahead. She had the prominent unfocused eyes and arched back of one impaled. In a few minutes she would be Mrs Tony. What would that be like? No one knew, yet.

There was a pause as the minister found his place, the tissuey papers whispering.

Ina felt an emotion rising in her, thrusting up from down deep. There was a moment, several long moments, when she knew that this emotion, whatever it was, would emerge, without having any idea what form it would take. Tears? A scream? A violent flinging of the hands? Something violent, anyway. Then she heard a low, harsh sound, like paper tearing. She saw the pageantry in front of her as a paper scene being torn, before realizing that the sound was coming from her. The faces, in focus now, were shocked, incredulous.

She, Ina, was laughing. A hard, calculated-sounding cackle that filled the small church. She was laughing at Nancy's wedding and she couldn't, wouldn't, stop.

Uxorious

SHE WILL TELL HOW he used to watch as she walked down the street to the bus stop, his face hanging in the window like a mini-moon. Sometimes it wasn't even dark yet, she will marvel. Marvel and also despair at, in the mingled tone in which people speak of Shakespeare or of saints, as miracles they have had to acknowledge. I was a lazy bum, she declares, but he picked up after me. He cooked and cleaned and did the laundry, and it wasn't because he liked those things. Believe me, he let me know. When an alert listener pounces on this evidence (as a sceptic might pounce on a slack line or a recorded cruelty), she answers, Oh, yes, we fought. She chuckles quietly at some memory. We yelled with the best of them. Even threw things. But you know, sometimes even then, he would pause, and get this funny half smile on his face, like he was remembering how happy he was. That usually made me madder. People at the reunion are listening now, and not asking any more questions. You can tell she's in her element, displaying this adoration she once commanded, but still in enough awe of it not to exaggerate. It happened to her: that's what she can't get over. She pauses. Says quietly, He liked all of my smells. Glasses freeze in mid-air. *All of them.* After a bit of fidgety silence, the tension pops. That must be love, someone says, and everyone, she included, laughs too heartily. But now a groove is laid down, and drinks, lovers, later, she comes back to it. Saying, He still went down on me after he knew I was seeing other men. His tongue where they were. The last time we were together, he was making me come five minutes before I left. She is drunk now. We all are a little. Among the people who are left there is this embarrassed yearning silence, like you might find in a small tour group in a cathedral, trying to imagine the people who would build such a place or worship in it. Melancholy lowers over us when we can't visualize ourselves inside this kind of space. I can't even recognize myself.

Sky Candy

HALLOWE'EN. Neil is due out on a weekend pass, which by now no one expects to turn into a discharge. Marisa and I get the spare room ready for him. The Bunker is where we hole up the night before exams and due dates; it is grim, littered with essay plans and rough drafts, but we keep a futon and a sleeping bag there to crash on. The stuff that was found with Neil in his apartment is in a stack of boxes in the corner. Neil likes it. He says the scraps of paper remind him of a mouse nest. On another visit he said he could hear the pages talking to him.

That's the kind of comment that irritates me.

'I hope he doesn't listen to my group dynamics essay,' I said to Marisa later that night, after Neil had dropped off and we were smoking a joint in bed. 'That would fuck up anyone.'

Marisa just smiled, exhaling. She is as patient with Neil as if he were her own brother, though I sometimes get spooked, just a little, by the idea that she is drawing on the same well of understanding when she deals with both of us. Like tuning in to the same channel, just a little louder or softer.

The weed helped. While Neil snored in a drug-induced coma next door, we sucked and held, and blew out the open window. Eventually, we made love, a hazy sort of pot love out of odds and ends of awareness; I remember it because afterwards Marisa hugged me hard, and said, 'Your mom and dad are so proud of the way you take care of Neil.'

That sobered me like a police siren, leaving me with a pulsing headache instead of a stone. I understand Marisa's point of view. We began seeing each other two years after my parents' closed-casket funeral. She has heard my stories and looked at my photo album, so in a sense, Mom and Dad are no less alive to her now than they ever were; but it bothers me to hear her talk about them as if they are still circling that airport in Houston, watching us as they wait for permission to land. I can't skim the next page of the story. The one where they feel a sudden jolt, hear a voice of false assurance, and plummet out of our lives. I was still in high school then – adrift in adequacy, as Dad feared – and Neil, the 'terribly talented' one, was close to graduating from the Ontario College of Art. Over the years, Mom and Dad had made their peace with his moods, shrinks, and pills – 'the artistic temperament' being a phrase they reached for often – but I didn't like to think of them hovering, helpless, as he quit school and dedicated himself to the secret art projects he called his Diagrams and Forms.

'There are no parents in heaven,' I mumbled into Marisa's curved back. But she was already breathing heavily.

Friday afternoon, Neil is in a bad way. He sits like a piece of meat beside me as we drive home from the hospital, mumbling yes or no to all my attempts at conversation. His head, when he moves it, suggests in an uncanny way that he doesn't care what his eyes are seeing. Slow, smooth, random arcs.

This is my brother, I keep thinking. As I battle the rush hour traffic up Jane Street, it becomes the dominant message I am sending to the other drivers, a précis of the usual braking and acceleration, honks and hand signals. *This is my brother.*

Marisa hugs him at the door, and he returns a rubbery smile, like someone trying to work the freezing out of his mouth.

'How are you feeling?'

'Okay.' His standard answer these days. Its only variation is *well*, which is ominous.

'Anything new on the drug front?'

He shakes his head no.

'Still on the Haldol, three times a day?'

'Yeah.'

'And the Cogentin?'

'Yeah.'

'No new side effects?'

'No.' With a goofy grin. Is he playing with her?

'Let's see your hands.'

He holds them up. His fingers vibrate with a fine tremor, like spindles on an idling motor.

'Okay, put them down.'

He raises them: The Mummy.

'I said down!'

Marisa's Big Nurse routine would worry me more if I didn't see how it relaxes Neil. *The fine line between comfort and dependence.* The sociology class that gave us that quote is where we met.

Neil shuffles into the living room. He drops with such finality into the couch that, for once, Marisa and I both stay in the kitchen to work on supper. Usually, by unspoken agreement, we keep a rotating watch on Neil and the balcony, one of us always in the room with him. We are, after all, fifteen floors up.

After dinner, Marisa brings out the pumpkin she bought. 'Here he is,' she beams, hugging and patting her orange gourd, thumping its ribs.

'I'll do the sloppy work,' I volunteer, and get down on my knees on the newspapers Marisa has spread out. Marisa and Neil sit at the table with crayons to design a face. Using a serrated knife, I cut a circle around the stump of stalk, lift out the top, and begin scooping the stringy innards into a pot. Marisa plans to roast the seeds. The work is restful, pulling the cool slime out of its dark home, tugging and snapping. Up above me, I can hear Marisa urging Neil to 'Go for it. Let's have the wickedest, weirdest one ever.' Looking up, I see her sitting close to him, like an occupational therapist. As she sketches, she tucks her fine brown hair behind her ear – one of those routine feminine adjustments of the body in space – and beyond her profile I can see the spiky, unwashed spears of Neil's hair, his mouth ajar. The sight of these two people I love, brought together because I love them both, is suddenly so moving that I gulp, my eyes stinging. Furiously I scrape the pale rind.

Neil comes up with nothing better than a toothless cyclops – circle over oblong – so we settle for the usual triangles and fangs.

As I am cutting them out, he says flatly, as if just making the connection, 'Trick or treat.'

'Not this year,' I tell him. 'The super has banned it. Too much vandalism, he says. Instead, there's a box in the lobby that he'll distribute himself. Any tenant can contribute. So far we have, what,

Marisa? Some of those Wal-Mart kisses and gumballs?'

'Gumballs,' Neil echoes.

'It's ridiculous,' Marisa says, with feeling. 'I'm going out tomorrow to buy some real candy.'

'Fatso will probably eat it himself. Sitting there with his shotgun.'

Marisa chuckles, and Neil smiles glassily.

I set the carved pumpkin on the coffee table. Marisa lights the candle and turns off the lights, and the three of us sit on the couch in the dark, watching the flickering features. Not spooky, necessarily, but suggestive. A few minutes of the dark silence puts Neil under – his snores are like purrs beside me – and Marisa bundles him off to bed. I turn on the TV. When Marisa returns she blows the candle out. For some reason, though, neither of us moves the jack-o'-lantern out of the way. We have to shift apart and peer around it, like a fat head in a theatre. A fat, orange, empty head, that would rather leer at us than watch the show.

It is one of those nights where we never touch the remote, sitting through reruns numbly until a test pattern tells us it's time to go to bed.

Next morning, I wake up with a start and a panicky feeling of things undone. My dream of someone trying to wake me up gives way to a memory of Marisa shaking me and making me promise not to fall back asleep.

Nine-ten. No sound.

First thing, I open the curtain to check the balcony. Empty. Nothing but blue sky past the rusted railing, a banking plane. But then, what else could I expect to see unless my timing was perfect? We live in the heart of Downsview, near the juncture of highways 400 and 401. Farther west is Pearson Airport. Everywhere I look, on land and in the air, there is motion. When I slide open the window I hear a vague rushing sound, like pouring sand.

I part the door to Neil's room, enough to see he's still zoned. I remember I used to love it when Dad would sleep in occasionally and get up saying he'd slept the sleep of the damned. It made me feel safe, somehow. But then I entered into my logical phase and wondered, why would the damned be allowed to sleep?

Out in the kitchen, there's a note from Marisa saying she's gone to the library and to do the shopping, she'll be back by three. Six hours alone with Neil. But she's also brought in the *Globe*, it's on the counter, and for an hour or so I skim-read it, bouncing between 'World News' and 'Focus'.

When Neil plods out, I fix coffee and corn flakes for us both and sit down with him in front of the Saturday morning cartoons, gladly moving our sad, staring pumpkin to make room for our cups and bowls.

We talk, sort of.

The little I know about art I got from Neil. I used to love watching cartoons with him, hearing him scoff or marvel at someone's line or shading or characterization. The fact that he wasn't lecturing me or showing off, was only murmuring to himself, made it seem all the more like privileged information. But now, when I feed him cues about what I think I'm seeing, he only has the same bland, even praise for everyone.

'It's well drawn. They're all good artists.'

He watches, it seems to me, the way an amputee would watch a sprint by his former teammates, with a final, terrible appreciation for muscle. Except that there's nothing terrible about Neil's appreciation; there's no rage or self-pity, or his old scorn or wonder, in his face. Nothing but a slack gape of amusement – at drawing! It's the drugs – which I'm not saying aren't necessary. They've made the world so unfathomably complex and out of reach that he can only stare at the passing show, milk dribbling onto his chin, like a baby needing a shave. Or is it the drugs? Christ, I don't know. No one does.

Once, watching him do a seascape in watercolour, I asked him what a 'wash' was.

'Anything from a heavy fog to a light dew,' he said, without pausing in his brushstrokes.

I backed away, happily baffled. There is a certain age when all you ask from an older brother is that he amaze you. Stagger your mind with unexplained exploits. But that age passes.

Gargoyles roam for half an hour, fighting and leaping among the skyscrapers. Then X-Men, more mutant outcasts. 'Life with Louis' is a change of pace, a satire of family life that seems to bore Neil altogether, at least until the point on the father-son fishing trip where the lummox dad gets dragged overboard by a feisty fish.

That trips something in Neil. You can see his mind rise, his face come alive around an idea or recognition.

He turns to me. 'You remember that time you caught that pike?'

'Sure I do. Dad's Georgian Bay bass hunt.'

Neil doesn't smile. 'Tell me,' he says.

'You remember. We were fishing over a shoal and we'd caught a bunch of small bass. Then all of a sudden my rod tip just sank like a rock.'

'Yeah?'

'"That's no damn bass!" Dad kept yelling. "That's a lousy snake."'

'No more bass.'

'He wanted to cut the line. He was disgusted. He knew it was the end of the bass on that shoal. But you wouldn't let him. I could hear the two of you arguing while that pike was thrashing back and forth.'

'You were scared.' Neil grins, the first real grin I've seen in ages. He's sitting up straight, like he's got a spine again.

'I admit it. Hey, I was five years old. Maybe six. Even Dad said it was a big pike.'

'What did you call it? A ...?'

'A crocodile. After it tired itself out and it was just lying on the surface with its eyes out of the water.'

'Yeah?'

'Remember, Mom made a chowder out of it, and I wouldn't eat any?'

But Neil has stopped at some point further back in the story, or has made an abstraction of it. 'Fishing,' he murmurs, sinking back into the couch.

Fishing.

That's all he says, but I can see that something has hooked *him*. There's a familiar gleam in his eye, and I sense that something in the story will haul him to the surface no matter how much resistance the drugs offer.

Sure enough, as soon as the show ends, he excuses himself, saying he needs to do some drawing. Is there some paper and a pen he can use?

There's plenty of both in the Bunker.

After an hour, I can't stand it any more. I can hear mumbling that takes me back years to when his paintings would evolve as a three-way conversation between his hand, the canvas and himself as an impatient bystander muttering at both. I also hear clanks and clunks, and I know what that means.

In the Bunker, Neil is sitting cross-legged on the floor, surrounded by items he has pulled from his boxes. Cans, bottles, wires – irregular pieces of metal and wood and plastic. String, buttons, newspaper. Such 'found' objects were the raw materials from which the Forms were made. Constructions I never saw in their entirety, since Neil smashed them before turning the finer instrument of a razor on himself. He is still rummaging in one box when I come in the door.

'I don't have what I need,' he says, urgently.

'What don't you have?'

'I thought I did,' he says. On the floor is a page chaotic with lines and jottings, and I guess that I am looking at a fresh Diagram. He stands up. 'Can we go to a hardware store? Or a Wal-Mart or something?'

'Hold on,' I put up my hands. 'First tell me what's going on.'

His smile is mischievous. Superior, perhaps.

'Sure. Absolutely.'

And when he explains it to me, I'm relieved. It sounds kooky, sure, off-the-wall, but in a fun way, zany, not dangerous. Like the suggestive shapes he used to clip into the hedge at home, the two of us snickering every time Mom or Dad looked out the window, betting how long it would take them to notice. The old Neil. The balcony is my only worry, but I figure Marisa and I will be right beside him.

'I'm in,' I tell him.

Marisa is home when Neil and I return with our purchases: baggies, cupboard hooks, three spools of nylon fishing line. 'Twenty-pound test,' Neil insisted. 'We don't want to have it breaking on us.' And extra candy, lots of it. Fuck that fat old super.

Marisa has her doubts about the plan. She worries about the super, our lease; and I'm sure the change in Neil has unnerved her, too. I remind her of the kids.

'Well, maybe,' she comes around a bit, 'but I think I need a doob to really get into it.' We glance aside; she often says the same thing before we make love.

After our puff, we get busy helping Neil fill about fifty super bags of candy – mini chocolate bars, gum, liquorice, bridge mixture, suckers – the works – and twist-tying them closed. He works swiftly, despite his fumbling fingers.

After we each tie a cupboard hook to our line, Marisa wonders if, dull as the hooks are, we should still cover them with tape.

A shrill, juiced-up voice, which I recognize as my own, overrides her. 'They know how to strip the bait, right, Neil?'

'Right.' Licking his lips in concentration.

It is twilight when we finish, still a little early. Marisa lights the jack-o'-lantern, and its flickering takes on power as the room dims. This is the time when Neil, unable to join us as we toke again, flattens slightly, his Idea stalled so that all the forces countering it conspire to pull him down. He stares dully at the serving tray piled with candy bags, as if trying to fathom how they got there.

We sit there, not saying much, until we hear the first faint shrieks from below.

Fifteen floors up, there is almost always a wind, and it is a raw, clammy one tonight. Clouds tumble through the dusk. The weed has waned and I feel jittery – half from excitement, half from apprehension that this is all a bad idea – as I hook on a bag using the twist-tie loop at its top. Marisa, leery of heights, is fixing hers at arm's length. She never trusts the railing not to give way.

Neil is ready to go first, bag in palm, staring out over the light-speckled city like some monk with an offering for it. Planes twinkle like fireflies, arriving and departing in the darkening pink of the west.

'Ready?' he asks.

We nod.

And over the side they go, three sweet bags lowered down

through the night, past the oblivious or incredulous neighbours, towards the dark flitting forms below. Down they go, feeding out the line.

Down, down. Down from this windy, light-spattered space.

It *is* just like fishing. I see the connection Neil's mind must have made, and for an instant I glimpse the awful economy he must have lived by during those months when no one saw or heard from him, until a neighbour heard the violence upstairs and called the police. A time of Seeing, when the lines – the Diagrams – connecting all things became plain, and the patterns of their connection in the mind became Forms.

'Not too far,' I hear Marisa warn, her free hand tugging on the bottom of Neil's jacket.

He is leaning out over the railing, frowning down.

'They're swinging too much. It's the wind and the light line.'

I look over and see the bags describing wide arcs above the heads of two children who are chasing them, jumping and screaming.

'Let it down some more. Down,' Neil urges, unspooling line himself.

I do, and then I feel it. A tug. Pressure transmitted from far below up to my fingers. And then a sharper pull, and then –

Nothing. It is thrilling. Looking over, I see my line billowing free, like a single, tremendously long white hair.

'Hurry. Hurry.' Neil is already wound up and baiting his hook again. I look behind him at Marisa, glad to see her swept up in it too, her eyes shining as she winds with a beating motion.

'Look, trolling,' she says, and slowly swishes her spool back and forth.

'Still fishing,' I say, and loop my spool around the railing a couple of times, like reins in a western. Marisa giggles, her fair cheeks red. Neil glances over. 'Right,' he says, and I wonder with a pang if two people can ever see the same Form.

Cries, wind-torn, drift up to us from the children. Soon there is a bunch – a school – of them, criss-crossing and leaping like minnows in their excitement. Dark skimming smears, throwing off occasional gleams from their plastic masks and torn white sheets. Marisa says something and I see her pass behind me into the apartment.

Vision, I think, giddy with it. I put my hand on Neil's back briefly, so happy to feel his body warm beneath the thin fabric.

That is when I see Marisa in the doorway. Beside her is a uniformed cop.

'What's going on?' is his obvious question. He delivers it sternly, but with a faint suggestion of a smirk. He's young, not much older than any of us.

While Marisa melts from his side back into the room, I explain as best I can. It sounds ludicrous, infantile, as I say it.

'You're telling me what I can see. What I want to know is why,' the young cop says, but with the smirk gaining. He knows we're not razor or poison freaks.

'Just something to do,' I answer. 'An idea.'

'Whose idea?'

I don't say, I wouldn't. From a sudden anxiety about where he is, though, I turn slightly to take in Neil. He is staring down at the children far below, his line 'still fishing' beside Marisa's and mine. His knuckles on the railing are white. He is shuddering, quivering all over like a waiting engine.

'Who are you?'

'He's my brother.'

I turn back to the cop, and then, out of the corner of my eye, I catch sight of Marisa in the bedroom – suddenly, there is so much to see, to keep track of. She is hurriedly gathering up everything relating to the weed: baggie, roaches and clips, vial of oil, knives. Her face implores – something, someone. I watch her a second too long, and the cop's eyes follow mine. He says:

'Don't worry, it's not my call.'

I nod gravely.

'Still, a little scare never hurts.'

I think that's what he says. I don't hear him, not really, because I feel, all of a sudden, movement at my back. It galvanizes me. Instinctively I swing with my arm outstretched and my fingers clutching. They clutch air.

My gut swoops, and I know this is falling.

Down. Gone.

Yet Neil is not gone. He is bent down over our tray of remaining baggies. He stands up with it in his hands and begins tossing bags out from the balcony.

'Hey!' the cop yells.

Neil waves the tray like you'd wave a magazine at a fly, and the rest of the candy goes sailing out into the dark. There it goes, a flock of sweet pigeons, arcing and plummeting. In my confusion there is a calm spot where I can notice things such as the cop's neat, squared sideburns and the fact that Neil gave the candy enough lead time so it would hit the ground beyond the children.

But no, I think, as he drops the tray with a clatter on the balcony, they are coming from all directions. Any bag could be a guided missile. What place could caution have in a Diagram?

'You,' the cop points a quivering finger at Neil. 'Go sit down.'

Neil shoulders roughly past him, bringing the blood to the young cop's cheeks. The cop and I stare at each other for a few seconds, as if gathering our strength for what must come next. Then the apartment door slams, and the cop is gone after him.

All of a sudden, I find myself alone. With the wind and the twinkling lights. Through the bedroom window, I can see Marisa, sitting on the edge of the bed with her back to me. She often cries a little while after she has toked.

I feel myself alone on a tower, the mass of the building beneath me melted away to a simple platform. This can't be what Marisa means by 'watching from above'. It feels too curious and expectant, too full of fresh sensations, to be much concerned with what is happening below.

A shout makes me look down. Night has fallen. The children are no more than wheeling shadows, chittering around the larger shadow in their midst. Any moment now, I remember, another shape will swoop out from the shelter of the building, scattering them all.

Neil's shouts are louder and deeper than the others, but I can't understand them any better. I know what he wants, though. He is my brother.

One bag of candy, mine, still hangs suspended between the writhing filaments.

Looking straight out over the city, I free my spool and begin to unwind it slowly. After that first look down, I don't look again. Touch will tell me what I need to know. The fine cool line descends between my fingers, the weight suspended from it swaying like a pendulum. A regular transfer of weight, side to side.

I scan the limitless horizon. Stars glimmer in places through the cloud, like water droplets on a vast net. As long as I don't focus on any reference point for long, I am free to jump, to fly, towards the thin crust separating earth from sky. I feel my body lightening, draining its mass from my feet upwards. And then....

That tug. It is always exciting.

But this time it keeps coming. No release. No snap or surrender.

Breaking the laws of fishing, I think with a surge of panic. It will pull me down into its element or crawl upwards into mine. I hold the line with both hands at the level of my chest and lean back, hard.

Hard.

The line tightens, burning my fingers, and then, just as the pressure begins to seem bearable, constant as the ache of gravity, it snaps.

The Leaf Man

TODAY HE IS OUT in sleet. He works in any weather. My wife drops her pencil in disgust when she can't get her hands right. In Arles a woman turned 128 today. She's in Guinness now. She knew Van Gogh. Says she didn't like him. She was what, twenty, twenty-one? She sees a greasy guy with bad teeth, muttering to himself. The leaf man might be seventy. It's hard to say. He'll raise his head at a greeting, but he prefers to work. Head down, raking, sweeping, bagging. His own lawn, sidewalk, curb, then on to the next house. The angle of his porkpie hat is a constant. His clothes the colour of mushrooms, pants, windbreaker. His face the one time he brought it up looked like one of those dried apple faces, cracking as it shrank. It's a never-ending job, of course. Does he appreciate this or just accept it? Sometimes he'll keep on working even after the streetlights come on, stepping in and out of the smoky circles. We were surprised one day to see him on the bus. No rake or broom in his hands, just sitting there waiting for his stop. The day before the Arles lady's birthday the radio had a story about a Colombian man who lives with his coffin overhead, gathering dust in the rafters of his cabin. It seems he carved it for his eighty-fifth birthday, figuring he would need it soon. That was twenty years ago. I really can't stand to see him after a rain when a fresh load of wet leaves has come down. His movements, normally patient, become a bit frantic then. My wife has decided to give up on her hands and try something from a photograph. First thing in the morning, early as the birds, it's the sound I hear: whisk, whisk, whisk. Catching up with the night.

The Harvest Bin

ONE DRIZZLY SEPTEMBER afternoon, my wife phoned me at work and told me that our daughter had been hit by a car. I had been scooping millet from a sack into a bin in the bulk food store we own. Kate spoke in a wobbly rush, which helped me believe her when she said that Liz's injuries were not terrible. In a real crisis she gets steely-eyed and calm, and if she talks at all, it is to issue crisp reports. After I hung up, I telephoned our part-time employee, listening to the empty rings while I watched a yellow branch seem to shake itself in the rain; then I swung the sign on the Harvest Bin's door to Closed, and drove to the hospital.

In the emergency ward, a nurse directs me to a curtained cubicle down the hall. Behind the curtain, dressed and standing with her back to me, supported by new crutches, is Liz.

'Liz?' I say. I expected a bed at least, sheets, fresh plaster, if not an IV and a monitor.

'Dad?' she manoeuvres around on the crutches.

'Are you all right? What happened?'

'I'm all right.' But her lip trembles. This is my daughter: long-limbed and myopic, her thin nose barely a purchase for her large-framed glasses. She is eleven.

'It was so dumb, Dad. I'm sorry.'

Not knowing where I can touch her, where she hurts exactly, I lean forward and kiss her forehead. 'Shh. You're okay. That's all that matters.' Then I ask, 'Where's Mom?'

'She went to talk to the doctor.'

We share a smile. That doctor had better know his business.

Kate believes in the value of nutrition, of vitamins, of exercise, of moderate and regular habits; but the corollary of these convictions, I've learned, is a disbelief (or at least a stubborn doubt) that there are remedies of any kind. A customer will be inquiring about natural sources of vitamin B1, and Kate will say 'Thiamine?' and begin rhyming them off: 'Cereal grains, their outer coatings; green peas,

beans, egg yolk, liver,' until, halfway down her list, she'll say impatiently, 'It's all over the place,' her glum face implying that it may in
fact be nowhere. Her bustling work at the store is fired by a belief that
we are supplying a vital alternative to the large supermarket chains. To
me, it's a more practical matter. Some people want the President's
Choice and some people want tofu, and many people want both. Kate
and I were looking for a way out of our city office jobs when, on a
Sunday drive, an empty storefront hit us like a command: *Fill me or
forever repent*. We moved to Freelton six months ago.

The X-rays showed no fracture. The car, cheating a yellow light in the
drizzle, swerved to miss an oncoming car and skidded into Liz, the
fender catching her hip and throwing her several feet through the air
to land on a lawn. I see Liz flying, sailing over traffic, but my mind
cuts out before she comes down. Miraculously, though, she sus-
tained only a badly bruised hip and a scraped forearm. The driver, an
elderly woman, got out of her car screaming about the box that had
been on Liz's head, as if she couldn't be held accountable for a pedes-
trian who couldn't see properly.

'Why wasn't she on a school bus?' Liz screeches, mimicking.

Driving home in the van, the three of us turn the event over to
find more oddness in it, escapees from the land of tragedy into farce.
Even the autumn leaves seem comic, colours bobbing and dipping
as we pass. Kate looks at me, and I keep looking in the rear-view to
find Liz, propped up on her elbows along the back seat.

'Why did you have a box on your head?' I ask, again.

'It was raining.'

'So you put your head inside a box?'

'Not *all* the way.'

'Was anyone with you?'

'*Yeah*. Susan. She saw everything.'

'Why wasn't her head under the box?'

'She had her umbrella. She was leading me by the hand.'

'Oh, of course.'

Kate laughs behind her hand, and Liz lets me glimpse the silver
wire across her overlapping front teeth. An aura of strangeness sur-
rounds our words, otherwise so ordinary, as if the darkness of the

near miss has placed us upon a lighted stage, telling a fabulous tale.

'I kept the box. At the time I thought of it as evidence,' says Kate, shaking her head.

'Where did you say it happened?'

'Right at Mill Street and Lake. Just across from the McConnells. Susan ran home, and then Dee brought Liz over and drove us to the hospital. When I open the door, she's standing there with this humungous box and tears in her eyes. "Oh, Kate, it's Liz," she says, and of course the first thing I do is look in the box.'

Again, we all laugh.

'"No, Kate," she says, "I've got her in my truck," and starts bawling. Of course, nobody knew how bad it was then.'

'What came in the box?'

'It was something for Mr Hansen,' Liz says.

'Mr Hansen?'

'You know, the janitor. Something for his furnace.'

'What were you going to do with it?'

'Build a fort.' Catching my eyes in the rear-view, she adds, 'Like a playhouse. Susan and me.' Soon after we moved into the new house – which we call 'country' because it stands at the edge of town, on a long, partly wooded lot – I pressed Liz with the suggestion of a tree fort we could build together. A treehouse was a dream of mine as a kid, and I had found three perfectly spaced maples near the back fence. But the idea bored Liz; we bickered about it several times, until I let it go.

'Susan got a new piano. She's taking lessons,' she announces when we are almost home. Her dark hair splayed against the seat as she gazes out the window at the pitching clouds.

'You keep your cotton-pickin' fingers off my fruit, you young whippersnappers. If I catch you in my orchard again, I'll thrash you within an inch of your lives.' Liz's old scold is back, an aggrieved farmer now, railing at us in a shrill cracked voice as she brandishes the cane we found in a closet. Catching herself, Liz blushes fiercely and hobbles over to the couch to watch TV.

The cane, from an old sprain of mine, is really all she needs. When Kate helped her downstairs after her bath, I asked if I could see her injury. Liz looked aghast, but then, at a nod from Kate, she turned in profile to me and dipped the waistband of her pyjamas an inch or so, enough to show me a bluish hollow. 'It's way bigger,' she assured me, and I thought of a ton of steel striking my daughter's milky skin, her brittle bones beneath.

'Go easy. It'll stiffen up tomorrow,' Kate warns. Then kisses me on the forehead and heads off to the spare bedroom, our 'office', to write in her journal. Recently she told me, in a hushed voice, that she thought she had begun a novel. That intrigued me – how a daily journal could metamorphose into science fiction, which is all Kate reads and, presumably, would want to write – but by agreement I don't ask her about it.

I prefer doing the accounts at the living-room table anyway, glancing up often at the television. Distractions don't bother me, since I tend to work at things piecemeal, over long periods of time. I let the black-and-white entries suggest whatever they want.

We might have moved out of Toronto sooner, but Kate was worried about taking me out of the loop, letting me drift away from established friendships. Freelton isn't Siberia, I reminded her, but she felt a rural setting might encourage the development of a 'burrowing Selkirk', as she calls the men in my family. Our compromise was bulk foods. It seemed social enough. Scooping grains and spices from around the world, discussing the merits of wheat germ and brown rice with passersby – you can't be more in touch than that, surely.

What worries Kate is the family history. Dad's hunting shack at Black River, which even on off-season weekends always seemed to need repairs; my brother Ted's basement library, fixed up lovingly over the years with panelling, a couch and pillows, mini-bar and fridge, espresso maker – one improvement a year. Martha, his wife, calls it a slow-growing tumour. Mom just used to scowl, her arguing years behind her, when Dad stared out the window at the rain or snow and announced that he'd best 'pop up to the camp and check on things.'

My safety, I've always believed, is my lack of a ruling passion. If I did create a hideaway, what would I do in there? Dad had his ducks and deer and Ted has his detective stories. But I'm not an outdoorsman. I read a bit, usually library books that I return past the due date and pay a small fine. I have no plans to write a novel. Studying computer programming in the early eighties, I worried slightly that I was making my Selkirk exit, earlier than scheduled, into a small room. But Kate, the lanky redhead one screen over, who one morning brought two coffees to class, helped me to see it differently. To her, computers are entirely with-it, connected, out there; though I've never grappled quite as cleanly as she does to the new order: *web*, *net* – as if spiders were friendly, sociable creatures, or a tub full of minnows had chosen to squirm together.

And, after all – after a dozen years of shifting other people's data – we're here.

Liz got hit on Tuesday. Wednesday, normally a slow day at the store, is when we take inventory of stock; today, with Liz home from school to rest her leg, we decide I should stay with her. Kate can start inventory by herself. 'You'd probably just start thinking about her and lose count anyway,' she said at breakfast, and I looked up from my cereal, thinking that this was true but that in some way she was being unfair to herself; but she had her back turned, taking things out of the fridge.

Liz and I have a good, old-fashioned time together, making cocoa and playing checkers and hearts and double solitaire. I perform my card trick, the only one I know, which I have shown her about once a year since she was little. This time, she pushes her glasses up her nose and announces, 'I know how you do it.' From the start she insisted on figuring it out by herself.

'Okay, show me,' I say, sliding the deck across the table.

'I can't *do* it yet,' she frowns.

Overnight her muscles have stiffened, and she walks with a more pronounced limp today. 'No-oo,' she moans, though, when I ask if she needs an aspirin. Like her mother, she is wary of remedies; yet she suffers from many vague complaints – 'funny feelings', 'tingles', 'aches' – as if some cunning general sickness is shifting beyond description, and hence treatment. Sometimes it seems to me that a sort of fuzz, or pall, envelops my daughter, making her borders less sharp and clear than other people's. I can't quite see her, I think, or she has hidden herself from me; and other people might have the same difficulty, for I remember a series of her teachers struggling, on parents' night, to fill our fifteen-minute slot, after they had said Liz was pleasant and well-mannered and 'developing normally'. 'She's headstrong,' Kate will say, after a small argument, or 'She loves animals,' when Liz is feeding a few peanuts to a squirrel – as if, by these categorical and hasty conclusions, to bundle her into a more definite, strong-featured character.

After lunch, Liz gets dressed and we slip off to separate pastimes; she to watching TV while waiting for her friend Susan to come by after school, and I to do some yardwork.

Getting my tools from the basement, I see the cardboard box that figured in yesterday's mishap. It is a large empty box, the kind a new dishwasher might come in, with Murphy Bros. printed on the side. It looks odd, sitting on the concrete floor of the unfinished basement, as if waiting to be filled with the junk and odds and ends that surround it. This is what my daughter had on her shoulders, her head stuck inside? The idea is somehow tinged with scandal, with rampant mystery.

'I saw the famous box,' I say, upstairs, to Liz. 'What kind of playhouse are you going to make?'

'We *might* make a playhouse.' She is flipping through the soap operas with the remote.

'I'll help you paint it, if you want.'

'Okay.' As I am going out the door, she swivels on the couch. 'Can I go home with Susan to see her new piano?'

'Walking, you mean?' The McConnells are only four doors down. 'Susan can help me.'

'I don't see why not. But be careful.'

The yard is dizzy with slanting sun, one of the last good days perhaps, the drizzle that continued until morning still shimmering like dew. Our lot expands through phases of sodded lawn, then clumpy seed grass, and finally a band of trees and bush sloping gently down to a creek. The former owner seems to have laid in just enough sod to take him to the end of the cord on his power mower, since mine also runs out at the verge. After that, I use the whipper – an

L-shaped scythe that I swing like a golf club, flexing my knees and sighting to the flag – and clippers for the close work. I find yardwork pleasant enough in good weather, though I don't make the fetish of it some men do. Sometimes, last summer, on Sundays and my half-day off – this was after the store was up and running, which took less time than we had expected – I began haphazardly clearing brush among the maples and oaks at the back of the lot. You can barely see the house from back there, it comes to you in jigsaws of colour through the leaves. It was rough, sweaty work, lopping off random branches and pulling up plants I couldn't name by the roots, and I loved it. It was part of the house-pride Kate and I kidded each other about – sweeping just-swept walks, oiling hardwood floors like baby's skin. Spasms of ownership after our years of 'mortgage' apartments. I laughed at myself, taming my patch of ground. Finally, though, one day, I stood up, clippers in hand, and thought: I'm thirty-seven and I'm back here, whacking away. Why? That night, I took us all to Swiss Chalet. And I stopped brush-clearing.

Peering between the living-room curtains, I watch the two young girls go down the street. An average parent-voyeur, ready to disappear at a backward glance. 'Susan's the pretty one, I'm the nice one,' Liz says sometimes with a musing candour that makes me wince, especially since I realize most people would call bubbly, twinkle-eyed Susan the pretty one *and* the nice one.

My daughter, my daughter, I think, like an off-kilter heartbeat or her own three-legged limp, theatrically propped up by Susan who has her arm about her waist. The two straight falls of hair shine like seams of coal and pyrites in the sun.

It is no more than twenty minutes later that the phone rings. 'It's Liz,' Dee McConnell says breathlessly. 'You've got to come and see.'

My feet plunge into rubber boots and I lumber across the lawns, heart thudding. Seconds later, red-faced, sweating, shirttails floundering – desperate dad incarnate – I land at the bottom of the McConnells' basement stairs.

No one turns to look at me. They, we, are watching Liz, but a Liz none of us has ever seen before. A Liz transformed.

A Liz realized.

Luckily for Kate, I wait a while before phoning her. By that time I can tell her calmly enough what needs to be told, sparing her the panic I felt while reserving some of the surprise. Dee McConnell is a sobering influence, pouring tea as she babbles about tarot cards and ESP and faith healing, as if to tie Liz's metamorphosis into every unseen power she has ever heard about or possibly experienced. But every time I want to flee, as I usually do, from her sweet chatter into a bag of rice or a tub of peanut butter, that eerie echo from below – the sweet soprano with its dogged twin – pulls me back to where I am, above ground, hovering.

When Kate arrives after close-up, we are downstairs again, watching and listening. It irritates me to see how she is armed against the event, leaning back slightly from the waist with her arms crossed, as if her legs are pulling her down the stairs unwillingly. But soon, as she stands at the circle of space we have left to the two girls, I see her lips part, her shoulders slump and her arms relax at her sides. She seems to come into her lean body, occupying it fully. She looks older.

Can we really be the same two people who, not quite twelve years ago, fretted and giggled through a sleepless night, confessing their fears about a parenthood looming like a ship? And made careful love. And – one of them – cried. Those people seem to waver, not just in the fog of the past, but on an island of possibility cut off from the mainland of everyday fact. One day they rowed, or were blown, across from what-if to what-is, where they built a house from what they could find and salvage.

The old hooked rug the piano sits on looks like a raft that might make a trip in the other direction, back.

Now Susan has stopped singing the melodies that Liz picks out, tentatively but note-perfect, and she backs away from the piano, steps off the raft, as if to grant Liz her enchanted circle, her voyage alone. Liz, her hands poised on the keyboard, turns once to look at us; on her face is a complex look, puzzled and decided, that makes my heart ache.

Where am I? her eyes seem to say. Or, perhaps, simply, *Goodbye.*

She cocks her head to one side and moves her lips as she traces out the intervals of the melody with her fingers. The songs are old favourites – 'This Old Man', 'Twinkle Twinkle Little Star', 'Baa Baa Black Sheep' – as well as popular songs from the radio. The slowness with which she plays makes the melodies seem dreamlike, like movements underwater.

This is all brand new. Liz has given no previous sign of musical gifts. She has sung, in an average voice, along with songs she likes, and danced sometimes and tapped her feet. She has never asked to play an instrument.

No one speaks. Finally, Dee McConnell says, 'Oh, my God.' Then, as if a spigot of amazement has been tapped, she can't stop speaking. 'My God. Oh, my God,' she says after every cluster of notes; and then, 'It's like Mozart.'

I look sideways at Kate at this, hoping to share a smile. A good ear, even perfect pitch, is hardly Mozart. Besides, listening for a while now, I am hearing more mistakes, fumbled and corrected notes that my wonder blotted out. Liz's time, especially, is off, the right notes coming in strange spurts and halts, like the steps of an awkward dancer. Talent is what I see. Raw ability.

But Kate is staring, still in the realm of miracle. She makes an atheist's fierce course changes. Her mind will purchase this unknown painfully, remapping a familiar coast.

Finally, Liz raises her hands from the keys and gets up from the bench, backing away from the piano soberly, as if from a new master. She finds her cane, leaning against the wall, and limps mightily, exaggeratedly, over to us.

'I'm hungry,' she says. And I realize I am, too.

At home, Kate takes some stew out of the freezer to microwave, while beginning an argument with Liz. Liz and I are sitting at the kitchen table. I am sipping a glass of beer.

'Didn't you know you could play by ear?' Kate asks accusingly, as if she might have been playing sonatas behind our backs.

'I never played before.'

'You'll have to take lessons, of course.'

'I don't want to take lessons.'

'I wonder if there's a decent teacher around here. We might have to drive a ways.' Kate opens the microwave door and stirs the stew, then closes the door and pushes buttons; the machine whirs.

'What if I don't want to take lessons?'

'That's not even a question,' Kate says airily, knowing it is and will be. 'The question is, how are we going to afford a piano?'

I raise my hands in a conceding gesture.

'Did anyone on your side play?' Kate asks me.

'No one.'

'I didn't think so. Aunt Orelie plays, a little, but she never played by ear.'

Liz is staring glumly out the window, the tip of her thumb in her mouth. 'Can't I just play Susan's piano?' she asks.

'You're taking lessons,' Kate declares, not the end of the argument but the beginning of one so protracted it can be deferred.

Presently it catches fire again, sputtering on through dinner, and beyond. I move into the living room in front of the TV, and between the sober comments of Jim Lehrer and his guests, I can hear it latching on to other topics, old and new. Liz's hair, her homework, new shoes. These snippets summon a familiar sense of exclusion that is partly happy – a lone male looking in on an assured female world.

'No, I want to keep it!' Liz cries out suddenly.

Muttering then, an angry buzz. Kate's footsteps thump down the basement stairs, and I realize: *the box*. This is about the cardboard box.

I hold the television remote, not knowing whether to turn the sound up or off. Doing neither. Kate pounds back up the stairs, and there is a short barked 'No!' that sounds more like a seal than my daughter. Another muffled exchange, then a slammed door.

After a silence, Kate comes to the door of the living room. 'Come and see how our prodigy's regressing.' She smiles thinly.

Reluctantly, I follow her to the garage. Already I am prepared to cancel the performance in the McConnells' basement, to preserve my blurry Liz against this emerging, hard-faceted one; though I know this is treachery.

Behind the slammed door, the garage is dim, grainy with the dusk outside the single window. Liz is sitting inside the deeper dark of the cardboard box Kate has set beside the garbage. Her sore leg and the tip of her cane jut out onto the dirt floor. Within, I can just see her slender arms clasping her other knee to her chin, her dark eyes glowing.

'You're acting like a two-year-old,' Kate prompts, behind me.

But before I can pass on this accusation, I realize I don't believe it. Hiding in a box, or anywhere, doesn't seem particularly childish to me; only dangerous. So I say:

'Come out, Liz.'

She doesn't move.

I look over my shoulder at Kate. She shrugs, and suddenly I have the disconcerting sense that, of the three of us, I am the one who understands least about what is going on. Crouching down, I find myself inside the same bubble of trepidation – of ignorance cherished, perhaps – that used to waft me down the hall towards my father and one of his 'talks'.

But then, there is Liz – scrunched inside her cardboard cave, her face full of uncertain resolution and her glasses dangling from one hand to show she has been crying, and might yet. A child.

My child.

'Do you have something you want to do with the box?' I ask her.

No answer. She is looking past me, down at the dirt. 'Well, we'll leave it here until garbage day, then. If you decide something before Monday, you can tell us.'

Silence weaves between us.

'I don't want you to go away,' she says quietly.

'I'm not going anywhere.'

She darts a glance at me, seeking the reassurance in such a quick answer. Am I just parrying a child's fear, or do I understand that fear? I don't know myself. My mind feels empty, curiously wooden, though I hear myself asking a question.

'Is it moving that scared you?'

She nods slowly, her eyes big with tears.

I take her hand and stand up, letting her stay in the box. She can come out when she's ready, edge out of the dark on her own time. Standing there, I have a view of the yard, a darkening green sloping down into bushes, the trees standing still, like people uncertain. Kate has left the doorway. Liz's hand is like a kernel wrapped in mine, and it comes to me with patient swelling force why I cleared the extra space. Already I can hear the hammering.

When she was small, Liz used to end a sulk by inviting the person she was most angry at to take some unusual liberty with her, wiping away the hurt by a sudden, almost shocking, denial of herself. 'Swing me, Mom,' she'd cry at the playground, though she was afraid of heights and speed. 'You can eat my ice cream, I don't want it' – and she'd watch each mouthful of her favourite food disappear into my mouth.

So I am only half surprised when, after a few silent hours with her door closed, I come down the hall to find it wide open, and Liz in bed with her old tuck-me-in face on. 'My bruise is turning,' she says, invitingly.

Dizzy Lizzy, my dizzy Liz – could I go so far as to call her by her old giggly name, I wonder, going to sit on her bed.

With one hand she keeps the front of her pyjamas cinched up below her navel, while using the other to slide the elastic waistband down her hip, expertly revealing a patch of her bruise.

It has darkened overnight, from plum-blue to almost black. I stare at it, seeing the colours to come: the mottled purples, browns, that greeny-yellow. Muted, or murky, colours; cloaked or fading. The colours of dried fruit, with its soft collected lustre. They take me back to the first delivery by our major supplier, in April, a week before we opened. Kate was painting a wall, and I called her over to watch as I opened the top box. Figs, prunes, apricots, raisins – all in clear plastic bags, with twist-tie tops. So ordinary, so overwhelming. We looked at each other, smiling tightly, and then our hands crept sideways and linked for a moment.

In Florida

By moonlight, the drooping bellshaped flowers
hanging from a small tree are a waxy,
                                    khaki colour.
The banana tree's large fringed leaves, broad enough to
serve as roofing or an umbrella, shelter
the bright green fruit in a cluster just beginning to
                                    separate,
like a green hand forming, not a trace of IGA yellow.
Pines, palmettos. Amaryllis.
Hibiscus in luscious, postcard red, its stamens hungry-looking.
The spiky-leaved pineapple palm, its latticework
sides peeling off as it grows leaving smooth grey bark,
the shed strips lying around the base;
out of the tufted hair like excelsior a lizard
                                    crawls by starlight,
a retiree like me.

The Atwaters landed in Fort Myers at 7 p.m. After picking up their rental car, they drove to Punta Gorda with the windows down, exclaiming over the fact that they could do such a thing even though it was rather chilly. The air was moist and fragrant. Nan Atwater wondered if it could be oranges that gave it such a sweet, faintly citrusy perfume. Les said she was imagining that.

After a snack of Lipton's Cup-o'-Soup, they decided to take a walk around the compound. That was what Mrs Fairleigh, the owner of their 'unit', had called Sunset Estates when she gave them their key. 'She makes it sound like a prison,' Nan whispered as they left her door, Mrs Fairleigh shooting safety bolts behind them.

'It's what they're all called,' Les said.

'Or a barracks. Did you notice, her perfume smells like Lemon Pledge?'

Les pointed to some pale green fruits on staked trees about three feet high. The soil around the saplings was dark in the moonlight; it had been turned recently. Plastic name tags were affixed to the stakes. *Lemon, Date Palm.* Les read them out and they walked on. 'I don't think they needed to label everything,' Nan said. 'It's not a museum.'

Les nodded soberly. Patient and reserved by nature, he had become more so in his chosen career. For thirty years he had worked as an epidemiologist, someone who tracks the spread of disease and suggests ways of controlling it. He was trained to see trends, the big picture that might or might not lurk behind the single detail. That was why it was so alarming to him these days to find himself preoccupied with an isolated report. Front-line sightings led so easily to panic or denial. *They only had their arms around each other's waists,* he would catch himself thinking; *since when is friendship a crime? Fourteen. Fourteen's not a baby.* He was rationalizing and retrenching like an outback medic in the face of some startling symptom. But this was not Patient X, the carrier of a new or old plague. It was his son, Dennis.

The next morning, Les sat on the sofa and thought about what he might write. His hour was almost over. Nan had roughed in a sky. The only thing that came to mind was that he had chosen the wrong hobby, but he had already recorded that in an earlier entry.

Find a hobby. How many times had he heard that at his retirement brunch? Nan had got the same thing at the gallery shop where she had worked part-time. As if they were being advised to compose a last message to posterity. A parting shot. Nan began to paint pictures, watercolours, always of a lake or river, with a tree on the shore, and then, when she improved a bit, sometimes with a bird on the branch of the tree. Birds were hard. Meant to be delicate, flight-capable, they tended to come out as lumps, clods stuck to the scene instead of alighting on it. After flirting with woodcarving, gardening and French cooking, Les decided to keep a journal. 'Not a diary,' he told Nan. 'Who wants to know what I had for breakfast?' Each morning, for exactly an hour, he recorded his observations. He made some discoveries about writing. A description – of anything – started to sound like a poem if you broke up the line lengths. There were many things you could think but not write, since writing was a kind of doing. He tried not to censor himself, though he assumed he was.

'Finished scratching?' Nan called, and Les, smiling, closed his book. Her own hobby was *doodling*.

After lunch they took another walk. The sun felt clean, unreal, more Lemon Pledge. The compound was surrounded with high brick walls. Beyond the walls was Florida, its malls and swamps, too dangerous to explore except from a car. A woman with platinum hair and mahogany skin, wearing tight green shorts and a cerise singlet, nodded as she speedwalked by. Nan's raised eyebrow promised a name. Jiggles, maybe. Or Silicone.

Where the asphalt forked at a clump of palm trees, one side becoming a dirt lane that led, judging from the fishy smell, down to the docks, the Atwaters were startled by a large grey turtle that emerged from bushes and began crossing the road towards the seaward side. Its forelegs were like flippers, swimming across the asphalt; its rear legs were bowed and clomping, unclawed.

They stood for a few moments, watching it.

Les took a step, and the turtle retracted its head and stopped. When he touched the back of its shell with his toe, the head shot out, twisting back with a hiss. Les stumbled back with the look of comical shock that delighted Nan as much, and as often, as her names did him; not just his exaggerated fright, but his surprise at it.

After they had resumed walking, she remarked that the turtle's shell looked like a German army helmet. Les saw it instantly, wondering why he hadn't seen it first. There was a time when he had fallen asleep every night seeing those helmets, plus tanks, machine guns, all of it. He had been eight in 1939.

'Fore!' a man called, as a golf ball rose up from behind a bush and plonked onto the next lawn. Another ball lay near it on the grass; they nestled like two white eggs. Two thin tanned men in pastel outfits appeared, each carrying a single iron. They would be the chippers Mrs Fairleigh had complained about, her voice rising with the fear of broken windows. One man touched his cap at Nan. Their cleats clattered briefly on the pavement.

Two days after the Atwaters arrived, there was a reception for them and other newcomers. It was organized by the social committee and held in the lounge beside the pool. Scoping out the room earlier, Nan had seen bright blue broadloom stretching not quite to the beige walls, showing a border of bare concrete. A vacuum cleaner stood in the middle of the room, its cord running to the wall. Nan imagined a black woman eating her lunch somewhere. A bookcase with paperbacks had the look of being stocked by forgetful guests. Nan felt the emptiness of the room, like space she could touch. She shut the door and hurried out to the pool, with its tennis ball sun lobbed into blue, a frail old lady wading.

Now, however, the rec room was lively with conversation, two card tables jaunty with bowls of chips and peanuts. It was BYOB, but ice in plastic bowls and a generous selection of mixers had been provided.

The Atwaters joined a group near the mixer table that included another Canadian couple, the Garries, a stringy pair from Indiana called the Brittels, and a tall handsome man with thick grey hair and a sullen expression who was introduced by John Brittel as Senator Stone, from Wisconsin.

'I wish you wouldn't keep saying that,' said the senator. 'You know I lost the election.'

John Brittel shrugged, smiling. 'What can you do?' He addressed the four Canadians. 'It was the Democrats' year. Give Clinton two years to screw things up and then he'll be in again.'

This observation seemed to increase Mr Stone's sourness. He left to refill his glass, and Helen Brittel clamped a hand on Nan's arm. 'He's dying. Cancer,' she muttered, then smiled at the returning Mr Stone.

Nan, not knowing what to say, caught Sue Garrie's glance. She seemed to peep out from the shade of her large, quiet husband, Oscar. 'Wish we had anyone even half as good,' Sue said, adding vaguely, 'as any of them.'

The four Canadians nodded at each other but did not enlarge on the political situation back home. No one had asked them to. The three Americans were looking around the room.

'More fresh meat.' John Brittel shot an elbow at Les's side and gestured with his glass at the door, where another pale couple had entered and were in the process of being absorbed by a tanned group.

'Yes. I see,' said Les. Something in Brittel attracted him, some shrewdness, not without its cruelty, that was partly hidden by a jocular manner. At least, thought Les, he seemed to be making an effort to size up situations, to analyse them. His brain was working.

'Watch yourself in the sun at first,' Helen said to Nan, her talon-like fingers on her arm again. 'You'll see the locals in sweaters, they think it's cold. But don't be fooled.'

Nan nodded, grateful in the same way Les had been for the other woman's snaring certainty. Across the circle, which seemed already to have subdivided, she could see Sue Garrie trying to draw out the dying former senator on his political career, Oscar smiling and nodding above them.

They walked back from the party with the Brittels, whose unit was near theirs. The apartments were boxy but attractive, with white stucco walls and red tile roofs – 'Spanish,' as Mrs Fairleigh had promised. Unfortunately, yellow tape, like a police line, had had to be strung up on poles beyond the borders of flowering shrubs, after a botanically minded tenant had been nearly brained by a falling tile.

John Brittel walked with a cane they had not noticed during the social; it had leaned against the wall behind him and he had snatched it deftly when it was time to go. Why he needed it was unclear. He felt free to gesture with it, and moved it ahead with a little circling flourish in the air.

The Brittels declined the Atwaters' offer of a nightcap with wide eyes and windy renunciations.

'Don't tempt us!' Helen said.

'You settle in!' John ordered. 'You get a couple of old souses like us in the door and you'll never get to bed.'

Smiles went round the group. The Brittels said good night. They had only gone a few steps away when John hurried back, leading with the cane.

'How do you feel about fishing?' he asked Les.

Les said that he had done some, years ago.

'Check the local news tomorrow morning,' John advised. 'Bunch of us go down on the pier after sea trout. Come on down with us!

You get 'em when the tide's coming in or going out. Half hour before's when we start. Good night!'

He was on his way back when Helen Brittel skittered over to Nan. Nan smelled her stale breath and felt the imploring strong fingers; but Helen's eyes were warm under the streetlight.

'You a fisherwoman?'

Nan shook her head.

'Good! We'll get our beauty tan and have a little gab while the men catch dinner!' She started back. John was leaning on his cane, waiting. 'At the pool!' she called.

Les poured them each a rye and sat down on the couch with Nan. 'The Stayners again?' he asked, sipping. Nan smiled and shook her head: no way! This was an old joke, their tendency to pick up strays. It had begun on their honeymoon, forty years before, when a white-haired couple named the Stayners had monopolized their time. 'Do we look lonely?' Nan asked. Les shrugged; this too was an old question. They watched the eleven o'clock news, most of the half hour taken up with crime. There was a murder and rape in Tampa, along with several local beatings and robberies. The national news shrank to make room for it.

Lizard sentry,
2–3" long, mottled grey-brown, pops up
*   suddenly on the screen,*
standing erect and vigilant, head and one leg raised
*   like a pointer dog,*
tolerating approach within a certain range,
darting away when an invisible line is crossed.

Sipping coffee, preening full light.
Hope he comes back.
Waiting to tell Nan, still on the phone to Dennis.

Dennis is fine, sends love. No sign of him.
Continuing then: last night's scream, probably a bobcat;
the egrets gracefully stalking the mud flats at low tide,

fine white strands lifted
from the backs of their heads by the slightest breeze;

the pelican that landed on top of the condo complex
and made a series of interesting, quite peculiar silhouettes,
black, the setting sun behind him,
as he shifted in various positions.

In the night Les woke to the sound of Nan crying. Opening his eyes, he saw light leaking around the top and bottom of the bathroom door. It was where she usually went. She would be sitting on the toilet, a Kleenex held under her nose and others bunched in the hand resting, palm up, in her lap. He had only opened the door once, but the picture had branded him, its details seared across some tough hide in his consciousness.

He raised himself to a sitting position and put the pillow behind him. He switched on the bedside lamp and opened his Le Carré novel. The words swam and blurred; he was too tired to read. He stared at the lighted rectangle; when he heard the water run he narrowed his gaze. It was what she wanted from him. Not a hug, not comforting words, but the knowledge that he was similarly afflicted. That whatever was keeping her up had attacked him too. He listened. Her sniffling was faint and steady. Dennis.

Later, after they had both been reading for an hour or so, Les put down his book. He looked around the new bedroom, blinking. Concentrating on the story had not only brought him fully awake, but the print had become so vividly real that it had dislodged his surroundings. The letters were like little black rivets holding down a brilliant fluttering picture so he could see it. Now he turned from the picture to the shadowy room, as a painter might turn from an absorbing canvas to a studio in which dusk has fallen, and saw shadowy, ordinary things, slowly becoming familiar. A print of ibises. Floral-patterned curtains, vaguely vegetative swirls. The cushioned wicker chair and glass-topped wicker table Mrs Fairleigh was so proud of.

Here. In Florida, he reminded himself. Punta Gorda. Winter. Retirement.

Reaching for the lamp, he said, 'We better see about getting some sleep. John and Helen look like crack-of-dawners to me.'

'Hm. I'll bet,' Nan said, with her bracing hint of acid.

In the dark, Les found her hand under the covers. He had said the right thing at the right time. Marriage, he sometimes thought, the core of it, was the development of a language peculiar to two people, a grammar, a syntax, a rhythm, a vocabulary. Sometimes, communicating a great deal with a look or touch, or with silence, one could feel eloquent.

They lay in the dark a while like that, not speaking, Les's hand over Nan's, before falling asleep.

Dennis was their second son. Four months ago, he had been accused of pedophilia. No charges had been laid; only one incident, relatively minor, was known to have occurred, and the parents of the boy he had embraced at the chess club felt that further damage to their son could be avoided by 'low-balling' the incident. Les, struggling to meet Vic Brittmuir's eyes during their awkward coffee together, had to look away at this phrase. It made Dennis sound like a poor investment, a wrong turn – thoughts Les had had himself about his 'different' – 'arty', Nan said – youngest child. David, performing well at expected intervals, was the family's blue-chip stock.

Dennis was to seek counselling, for his alcohol problem as well as his sexual inclinations; this was the gist of the informal agreement that was reached in the Brittmuirs' den, Mrs Brittmuir, barred from the discussion of male aberrations, silently refilling coffee cups and then backing out of sight, like a butler in drag. 'Civilized,' Nan remarked, when Les returned home and told her. She continued cutting her potatoes into precise lengths, with a *thunk, thunk, thunk* on the cutting board that sounded like a fist upon a door.

Purely in terms of providing a focus during a blank spot, Dennis's trouble came at the right time. It came when Les was first beginning to feel the real strain of filling his days. Summer, though he knew he was retired, had felt much as usual. Then September and October had been busy, and had felt productive, as they planned their winter south. They did this conscientiously, comparing rates and climates, debating the relative virtues of Florida and Arizona and coastal

Texas, finally settling on Mrs Fairleigh and her 'lovely property'. That was when Nan began to notice the change in Les that she had been waiting for. It crept into his solid competence – a hint of vacancy, a befuddled air that offended her somewhat. Les had never been befuddled. Confused, yes, but that made him annoyed, not fussy and maundering like a forgetful housekeeper, taking much of the morning to follow a bran muffin recipe. He had even begun, quite suddenly, to walk like an old man, stooping a little and taking mincing steps.

Dennis's crisis seemed to jolt him back to himself. The evidence that he was still needed as a father in the original sense, as an adult responsible for a child, seemed to bolster him. It was his idea to invite Dennis to stay at home while they were gone, though he accentuated the 'house-sitting' aspect of the arrangement a little too heavily, Nan felt. Dennis was twenty-six. Their 'afterthought' – ten years after David – but hardly a kid. But Dennis agreed to stay, and sat quietly while Les went over the 'house rules', which Nan had to leave the room for.

Once, Les had visited the chess club, soon after Dennis had been elected president. Les had taught the game to his sons, but it had been years since he'd played. He went mainly in order to see Dennis succeeding at something. They met at Mother's and had a pizza together, after Dennis had closed Planets, the sci-fi used bookstore owned by his longtime friend, Martin. They walked up the street to the YMCA, and Les watched, pleased, as Dennis unlocked a games cupboard and directed several boys in setting up the boards and clocks and informed them about an upcoming ladder tournament. Other club members arrived and Les played a series of speed chess games with an old man from Eastern Europe who always lost on time but refused to set the clocks to a more generous interval. Near the end of the night, he took pleasure in being checkmated by his son, to the delight of a circle of onlookers. It was painful now to search his memory of those grinnning young faces for another reason. Thinking: That one? Or him? Him?

In the days that followed, Les and Nan noted the same linkings of tanned and pale faces they had seen in the rec room: swimming, taking walks, playing the chipping game, shopping at the mall. As it can at a dance, the accident of first-met seemed to lay down a law, a claim. Every group had its leaders, like the Brittels, and its followers, like themselves. And each group had a couple that Nan thought of as 'in reserve', like the Garries, people not unattractive, but not sought out. Even loners, like Mr Stone and his seldom-seen wife, orbited a particular group like moons.

News was exchanged, around the pool or on the dock, according to certain rules. Questions on both career and children were expected – to leave either out would seem odd – but they were handled differently. Detailed questions on one's former job, or 'line' as John Brittel put it, were welcome. Viewed under an earned sun, a job seemed a thing apart from oneself; one could rue it like rain. Sometimes, a former career offered a clue to a personality. Late in the afternoon, when the Garries had ended their shuffleboard playing and Sue had gone for a quick dip, splashing in the shallow end while exclaiming how refreshing it was (the other women watched her closely the first time but then not again), Oscar Garrie, wearing a faded brown outfit that looked as if it had been worn on many vacations, many walks along the beach, wandered over to the pier where the men were fishing to see what had been caught. He ambled along the weathered planks, pausing to look in the plastic pails used for bait and caught fish. Asking the name of a fish he hadn't seen before, and was it good to eat?

He stopped and stood behind Les and John. After a few moments, he said in a thick, slow voice, 'Watcha usin' for bait?'

Les, always quick to include an outsider, set his pole down with a clunk, and opened the lid of the shrimp bucket he and John were sharing. John had driven up to the bait shop in his Cadillac that morning. The shrimp were mostly dead already, pink-grey and strong-smelling.

'Shrimp, eh?' The large man squatted to see them better and Les was aware of a clean soapy odour coming from his close-shaved face, ruddy and large-pored. He saw his small, intelligent eyes taking in the shrimp with interest, fastening on them.

When Oscar had moved on, John said, 'He used to be a judge,' delivering the comment straight out at Charlotte Harbour.

'*Did he?*' Les said. It made sense. The slowness, the apartness, the settled habits. He saw the present Oscar sitting, in his comfortable chinos, behind a raised bench in an empty courtroom, his judgement suspended until it was needed again.

At the end of the pier, Oscar stood for a few minutes with his hands in his pockets, rocking back and forth. He put his hand up to see something against the sun. Cars crawled over the distant bridge; boats passed under it. Gulls wheeled and pelicans flapped up and dove down. He made a dark silhouette. After a while he passed behind them on his way back, his footsteps soft for a big man. Les saw him walk past John's Cadillac at the foot of the pier, his hands in his pockets, and disappear.

'A judge, eh?' said Don Rickert, a Pennsylvanian fishing on the other side of John. 'I imagine he's seen a few things, all right.' There was respect, perhaps pity, in his voice.

That, too, was apt: seen some things. An excuse, a condition and a privilege: it was all of these.

Children were another matter. Questions about them should be kept breezy, at first anyway. Children were not past in the way jobs were. Or, the happiest, simplest years were past, and the dangerous years were at hand. They were the likely occasion of griefs: divorce, mental problems, worsening habits.

It was Helen Brittel, on the Atwaters' second visit to the pool, who, in her bright, brassy voice, brought up the question Les and Nan feared and had not discussed.

'So, who's holding the Atwater fort back in Canada?'

The Atwaters could not look at each other.

'Well ...' Les began, and Nan jumped in.

'Two sons. Dennis runs a bookstore; he's minding the house right now. Mother's a little paranoid, don't you know. Our oldest boy, David, is an architect. Nancy and he live in Peterborough. Jacob, their first, came along about a year ago.'

Helen lifted her dark glasses slowly up her forehead and looked straight at them. Her arm was lifted as if to summon the attention of the other loungers. Les felt his stomach region go cold.

'Chips off the old block,' she said, incredibly.

Les could not look at Nan. Then, suddenly, he took in the meaning of Helen's uplifted arm. It was a gesture at the table between him and Nan, on which lay Nan's sketchbook and his own paperback. Instantly, his fear of Helen and resentment of her probing turned to admiration for her quickness, a respect that was close to awe. Sketching and writing: architecture and bookselling – why had his mind never drawn a line between these activities?

Energized by their relief, Les and Nan went for a dip. 'Race you,' Nan called, and was halfway down the pool before Les could mobilize himself. He almost caught up to her on the return, smacking the end of the pool with his leading arm and standing, winded, to hear the laughter and the cheers. John Brittel was squatting just above him, holding Nan's arm aloft. Blinking chlorinated water from his eyes, Les saw Nan smiling at him, heard the applause. Only former Senator Stone was still facing the other way, ignoring someone else's win.

———

Shrimp as bait, as food, turning pink-grey as they die.

The 'love bugs', flying in pairs joined at the abdomen; proceeding slowly and erratically, pulling in opposite directions.

(Nan is taking one of her 'wrist-savers', as she calls her breaks from her watercolours. Looking out the window towards the marsh, her hands on her lap. One advantage of my kind of painting: no one can tell you're not working, since thinking is half of it. I wish one of the lizards would pop up for her. Both our hobbies are coming along. She says her pictures don't look like anything. I tell her neither do mine – yet! Notes is a better word than poems, I think. Less pretentious. One possibly hopeful sign is that Helen says I look like the 'studious type'. So Nan says anyway. John just talks about money, his arthritis, and what bait works best. Good company, though.

Mr Stone was an odd duck. Nobody liked him much. That was why he was still called 'Senator', sometimes even to his face. By now this brought only a frown and a tired wave. He seemed vain, and his illness, which in another would have inspired sympathy, seemed part of his vanity. There was an ostentation to his stiff, wounded walk, the precise hours he spent in the sun, not reading, not talking, turning every few minutes, as if dedicated solely to absorbing whatever helpful energy the sun could offer him. His marriage was assumed to be bad, since his younger wife seldom accompanied him to the pool, preferring to shop with friends. She had been his secretary and had married him for his money; uncertain about his will, she was going to enjoy it now – the rumours began to arrange themselves in sequence.

One day, Nan ran into him in Publix. Les was next door at Eckerd's, checking the specials on pop and beer. Mr Stone nodded dolefully at her as she pushed her cart past his. There was something about him that Nan liked: his formality was like the portico to a mansion where one could stop and talk awhile, sheltered between the lawn and the door, close to both; though after noticing this attraction – really no more than the space where an attraction could exist – she had not thought about it further.

After filling her cart, she ran into him again. He was standing with a package of bacon in his hand, looking over it at other packages. Nan recalled that his wife's name was Zeeta. Tall and slim, he bent forward stiffly, the bacon slices near his chest. There was a solemnity, and an absurdity, about him. A natural gravity coexisting with a natural lightness – it confused Nan.

Dying alone, she thought, then frowned. No, that wasn't it.

Strange, she thought, how the dream keeps springing up with the oddest people: the dream of bypassing all the usual channels and ways and means of getting to know someone, of attaining limited knowledge of them, in order to find someone whom one knows at a glance, all through. No more steps, ploys, gambles, hard work: just communion. It was something like that, strangely enough, that she sensed was possible between Mr Stone and herself. Not romance, necessarily, though the dream could take that form: the dream of truly knowing someone. It frightened Nan.

Les was putting his stash of American beers in the trunk when she came out. Excitedly, they compared the deals they had found, exaggerating their pleasure unthinkingly. Bargain-hunting seemed an important part of retirement, a prowess that could actually grow with advancing years.

One raw day most of the regulars stayed away from the pool. Nan found herself alone with Mr Stone. He was lying on a chaise longue with a towel under his head and his eyes closed. He had on a short terrycloth jacket; goose bumps stippled his bare legs. Nan sat down at a table under an umbrella and opened her *Vanity Fair*, concentrating hard on an article about a dead model in order to block out the breeze. After a while she opened her sketchbook, thinking that a little activity might warm her up.

At a sound behind her, she turned. Mr Stone had swung his long legs over the side of the chaise and was sitting up, facing her.

'Homesick?' he said. After a moment Nan thought he might be referring to the coolness and the grey, scudding clouds.

'Oh, gosh no,' she said. She went on quickly. 'This is nothing. Back home, they'd give their eye teeth for a day like this.' She stopped, suddenly uncertain.

Mr Stone was nodding slowly. It was strange, the way he was looking at her: just looking, as he might look at anything that interested him. Nan became embarrassed. *He hasn't got long*, she found herself thinking; and at the thought his face became decipherable. He was lonely.

'We've been talking for two minutes and you haven't asked me about my political career,' he said with a faint wry smile.

'I'm sure you've heard enough about that.'

'And you have, too.'

Nan laughed nervously. 'We do go on here, don't we?'

Mr Stone reached up and rubbed the back of his neck. The cloth jacket parted to show more of his slim brown chest with its long silver hairs. 'Or my health?'

Nan blushed. 'That's your business. I am sorry you're not feeling well.'

Mr Stone nodded slowly again. Looking up at the sky, he asked, 'Canadian discretion?' A glance at Nan. 'Like Sue?'

Nan shrugged. Sue Garrie was a mouse.

Mr Stone puckered his lips as if tasting something piquant and arched a silver eyebrow. For a second, his face was lively.

'I appreciate it anyway,' he said. 'I'll let you in on something. I was

thinking of retiring before they threw me out. I actually feel quite
well, probably better than I have in years. When does someone stop
"having" cancer anyway? Two years? Five years? It's been eighteen
months since my treatment stopped and I feel fine. Oh, and ... my
marriage isn't in trouble. It's over.'

That was mean, Nan thought. After all, she *hadn't* asked. But no
doubt he was used to being in charge. Events had bullied him, and
he was using her to dust himself off. She didn't mind, really. There
was a transparency to him that she associated with all politicians, a
kind of innocence. People obviously playing a deceitful game sometimes, in certain lights, looked clean; the way on a camping trip you
washed the plates with sand, what you called 'dirt' at home. It was
his blank face that unsettled her. Expressions that used to live there
had departed. Would it stay empty, or would something else move
in? Her sketchbook tugged at her arm, a dull friend, but she would
take her chances with Mr Stone.

They chatted about vitamins and Robert Ludlum. Mr Stone
adjusted his chair to a higher position and leaned back, smiling at the
sky. Nan sensed she was being charmed. Flirted with, she thought,
enjoying the absurdity of the idea. Zeeta was at least fifteen years
younger than she was.

The sun appeared after a few minutes. The clouds were breaking
up. Sue Garrie came out of the change room and began splashing in
the shallow end. Helen Brittel entered by the gate and, pretending
not to notice Nan and Mr Stone, sat down some distance away. Nan
caught the senator's cocked eyebrow. Then Sue, meek and dripping,
poking a towel at herself, trotted by with a fawning smile and sat
down beside Helen. Nan heard bits of an anecdote about a black
saleswoman with a notorious temper, and Sue's appalled 'Oh!'s and
'Oh, no?'s, along with nervous giggles.

At the same time, Les was coming to the end of his tenure as John's
fishing buddy. He had seen something of the sort on its way: the
Brittels liked to 'make' friends rather than find them; but he had
expected them also to need to keep friends once made, and so to prefer a fade-out rather than a rift. But something happened to force the
issue.

They had caught three sea trout that day, which were in the plastic pail between them. They were joking about how pleased Ron Dinkins would be – a non-fisherman who loved to scrounge extras – when something took John's shrimp and headed towards the middle of Charlotte Harbour with it.

The line sang out with a whine. John set the hook once, twice, as the nylon streamed out. Flustered, he scrambled to his feet, shooting out a leg that knocked over the shrimp bucket; for the first time, he looked crippled. He held the cork butt of the rod against his belt, unused tendons standing out along his thin forearms; his face was red. He leaned slightly in the direction away from the one the fish was running in, a spurned suggestion.

Les saw a huge grey shape, deep down in dark water, propelling itself away from the shallows where it had felt a sharp pain.

Footsteps banged on the wooden walk. Art Buck and Don Rickert had left their poles and come down to see what was happening.

'Shark, maybe?' Art Buck said, behind them.

'Gotta be,' John puffed, jerking at the drag star with his thumb. 'I can't even turn it.' He sounded incredulous.

'Careful, J. B. That's Ron's dinner,' Rickert chuckled.

'There's lots of big fish,' Buck said. 'A snook might be able to do that. A big one.'

'I must be almost out of line,' John said, trying to peer inside the reel while holding the bowed rod.

'Hey, hey,' said a familiar deep voice. Les glanced aside and saw Oscar Garrie looming, looking less phlegmatic than usual, his interest piqued. *This* was evidence.

In snapping the line, the fish almost took John over the railing. He had succeeded in tightening the drag to the point where the rod was almost wrenched out of his hands. Clutching it, he gave a small yelp. Les shot out his hand and grabbed him by the belt. The cane fell into the water. He pulled John back. 'Jesus Christ!' John said, staring at his reel.

Art Buck used his rod to steer the cane down the length of the pier to the shore, where Oscar Garrie could reach it. Garrie swished it back and forth in the water to get the mud off.

Les had an extra spool of line which he gave to John. The incident began to recede. Except that Les could tell something had changed. It was so strange, the quickness of it, but he felt he was right. He was being phased out. More curious than hurt, he wondered why. Was it the hand on the belt, John's momentary helplessness? Anyone could be. But John had been. An encounter with a fish like that changes the nature of fishing, the roles being played. At the same time, Oscar's sluggish personality had finally been mobilized. He was asking John questions about fishing, and John was answering them thoroughly. Les felt he was seeing the groundwork of another alliance being laid.

Later he said to Nan, who had heard all about John's 'whale', 'I think the Stayners are about ready for bed.' Forty years before, the old bores had eventually nodded off, leaving the newlyweds alone.

Nan was in the kitchen mixing up some Quaker muffins. 'I hope so,' she murmured.

A few days later, walking home from the dock, Les saw Helen and Nan crossing the road up ahead of him. He hesitated, then called, 'Hello, ladies!' Knowing John was right behind him.

The two women turned. Helen dug her elbow at Nan's side, saying something that made them both chuckle. Les shook his empty stringer. Helen laughed harder but Nan only shook her head. It struck Les that he had married the right woman.

The turtle that Les and Nan had seen before moved out of the bushes and began crossing the road. Its leathery grey legs swept out slowly from its sides as it carried itself across the road in short stages that were like successive heavings of itself. Despite its bulk, it was almost silent.

Hearing the surf sound of John's Cadillac behind him, Les moved over so that he was standing between the turtle and the car. Nan came and joined him. These actions, which in retrospect seemed so deliberate, did not feel that way at the time. The Atwaters merely gravitated to where they were needed.

The turtle had stopped. They stood behind it.

Behind them, the Caddy's electric window whined down. John called sharply, 'Helen!' Helen Brittel appeared flustered for some moments, then went to join her husband. She gave the Atwaters a wide berth, walking on the grass to avoid them. Her flip-flops smacked against her soles. The Atwaters heard a crunch of gravel as John backed up to take the other road around the palms. Nan glanced behind her and saw Helen jogging to catch up to the car. 'Come on!' she heard. The door slammed.

Then the Atwaters were alone. They did not look at each other. They watched instead the turtle, which, with its limbs and head retracted, resembled more than ever an army helmet. An old grey army helmet left in the middle of the road, which it had somehow become their important task to guard. It was not necessary to ask themselves why.

Les touched the back of the turtle's shell with the toe of his shoe. Nothing happened. He touched it again. This time, the head shot out with its wet hiss.

'Oh!' Nan exclaimed, as Les stepped back.

He prodded the shell again and the same thing happened, except that the hiss was more insistent and prolonged, the beak swifter. Now Les grunted, 'Oh!' Nan, annoyed with him for touching the turtle again after the first warning, said nothing.

As they stood there, in the middle of the dusty road in the pink light of the waning day, they felt a quiet victory in what had just occurred. Each, for the first time, felt that the trip might prove to be a success; that, finally, sufficient grounds had been laid down for the retirement to proceed. Each suspected the other of feeling the same sense of triumph but they did not look at one another. It was easier to share the feeling by looking at the road.

Ink-stained

'I'M AN INK-STAINED WRETCH,' she used to say. And he thought of Othello's cry: *Excellent wretch! Perdition catch my soul but I do love thee.* She couldn't keep the ink, or anything she was working with, off her. Hands black as a grease monkey's after fiddling – her word – with the Vandercook press. Cranking words, invitations, programs and pamphlets around the cylinder. Half of it stayed on her. Black ink ground deep under her nails and forced into the wrinkles over her knuckles, smoothing them. Washing hardly helped. Her hands grained grey long after gardening. Orange-red palms two days after making catsup. Everything stayed with her, whether she wanted it to or not. He'd hand her an article on a transvestite Thai kickboxer that had interested him, and she'd say 'Hm', but an hour later, when they'd both moved on to other things, he'd notice the fine smear of newsprint still on her fingertips. Like butterfly wing dust, except that the world was the dusty flitting wings and she the casual fingers. Marvelling a bit, he'd leave for work, a volunteer project he'd found, helping an autistic boy learn passages of poetry, one slow line a day: *And when I love thee not, chaos is come again.*

Bitter Lake

WINTER CAME TO THE RESERVE the first weekend in November, just as Tremaine's last box arrived at the Bay. The cold came down like a lid with a hinged spring, a cold *snap*. The thermometer another teacher had left outside the window read minus 35 degrees Celsius. Friday night, Tremaine felt its approach in a clearing and thinning of the air; the heat vents blew harder. After dinner he turned the kitchen light off to discourage the kids and sat reading by a lamp in the back room. Several boys – he recognized Emmanuel and Joseph's voices – ran round and banged on the window behind the closed curtains. A new trick; just when he thought his message was getting through. He sat still. Simon, the caretaker, came out of his shack and chased them away.

The next morning, when he turned on the tap in his kitchen to make coffee, the water emptied out of the line with a small creak. No more came. He went into the other room. Behind the teacherage, the new principal was talking to Simon by the pumphouse. Breath steamed out from Al Sonder's parka hood, crystallizing on the fur. Simon ran a bare hand back and forth above the pipe, as if patting a giant dog, to show that there had not been enough snow to insulate it. Behind them, Tremaine could see how overnight the lake ice had lightened, whitening as the water receded beneath it.

At the Hudson's Bay Store, he bought what he could find that was not too expensive. When he had arrived in August the prices had outraged him, but over time outrage had moved back a few paces and drawn a new line. Two or three times the prices he was used to was now acceptable, quadruple was too much. He bought ground beef, flour, butter, potatoes and a bag of carrots. The apples were mush but he found a bunch of green bananas not too banged up. Bananas were an odd choice of fruit to subject to multiple plane trips and hasty loadings and unloadings, he had seen boxes tossed ten feet through the air, but it never paid to subject the Bay's policies to too much scrutiny. On one trip the freezer might be full of sirloin steaks and Haagen-Dasz; on the next, wieners. Daly, the gruff manager, said he ordered what the people wanted. Tremaine had given up trying to decide if the remark was inscrutable or just stupid.

Around him milled the dark faces of the townspeople, picking over the items or just strolling about the four aisles, as city people would do in a mall. Some greeted him, with a nod, 'Hi' or '*Bojo*'. Students from his class played a kind of hide-and-seek with him, pretending to ignore him or giggling behind small brown hands. Trips here, or anywhere in the town, seemed like an extension of school life; Tremaine tried to keep them short.

Daly waved him over to sign for the box his wife had sent. 'Cold's a bitch, idn't,' he said.

Nodding, Tremaine looked around. Several of his students had swung with him to the counter. They were watching him listlessly, hoping he would receive something, do something. As always, their boredom communicated itself to him, numbing him. Frederick Williams picked at a poster of Arnold Schwarzenegger, tracing the muscles with a dirty finger.

'Henry'll take it out back. Save you a few steps,' Daly said as Tremaine fished a pen out of his layers. Over the portly manager's shoulder hung a blankly virile brown face, one of a series of young men Daly couldn't keep.

'What you got, Don?' peeped a small voice as Tremaine gathered up his groceries.

He turned and saw Mary Ellen Mathias clinging to the wire holders on the video carousel, her small face with outsized glasses bizarre amid the Adult and Horror cartons. A naked woman astride a chair perched above her frizzy black hair.

'Groceries, Mary.' He knew she meant the box.

'Is your wife sends Christmas presents?' Mary Ellen hid a giggle behind her hand.

'I'll see, Mary.'

As he went to the cash, she darted behind him to the counter. Martha Wasoon, back from high school in Thunder Bay and the subject of many of Mary Ellen's crayon portraits, was next in line.

Mary Ellen and her sister Lucy, in the other class, stood out from the other students. They had pale skin, like a white person's, with button noses not typical of Ojibway faces. They were fragile, too, often away from school with earaches or colds; at recess they got teased for being timid and clumsy in games. At some point every day Mary Ellen approached Tremaine with brimming eyes and a trembling chin, complaining of a 'hurt' or somebody who had said mean things. Sometimes he turned at a barely perceptible touch on his hip and found her holding on to his belt loop. Involuntarily, as a weapon against the tenderness she evoked in him, he had developed a detached, firm way of speaking to her. 'You're okay, Mary,' he would say, patting her a little impatiently on the back or arm.

Halfway back up the road, the box on one shoulder, he remembered that he had left his Bic pen on Daly's counter. With a grimace of impatience he decided not to go back for it. Three boys with broken hockey sticks were chasing snowbirds from the vacant lot beside the school. Their sticks still raised, they ran at him.

'What you got, Don?'

'Some of my things, Roy.'

'You get big box, Don, man?'

'Yes, Jacob.'

'What's in the box?'

'I don't know yet. I have to open it.'

'You don't know what you got?'

'Not yet.'

The repetitiveness of his students' conversation, which tired Tremaine, also mystified him. He knew it was not due solely to their limited command of English. Or to their shyness, their insecurity not helped by the small number of outsiders they had spoken to in their lives. It was more than that. They took some comfort in getting him to say the same things to them over and over, marking a small circle of ground with indelible chalk. In his more depleted moments, Tremaine too found it satisfying: exchanges less like news than like a lullaby, like surf.

One of the big village dogs, mangy wolf-like creatures that had frightened Tremaine when they snuffled him the first day, came loping out from behind the radio station. Roy raised his stub of stick and the animal cringed, slinking away with backward glances.

'Scared cat,' Roy grinned. The other boys were smiling white smiles, too. Good-looking boys, with thick black hair. Then they ran away, shouting at the snowbirds that had landed again.

Tremaine had slit open the box and was reading Becky's letter, when he looked up and saw Roy's face squashed against his kitchen window. He laughed, then remembered that Roy was almost fifteen. Fortunately he pulled back from the glass without sticking to it.

'You got things?' Roy shouted.

Tremaine nodded, wondering whether Roy's energies could be subdued enough to help him unpack the box. Suddenly, though, Roy lunged sideways; Tremaine heard him clomping down the boardwalk to visit Al Sonder. A circle of freezing saliva remained on the pane. You couldn't escape the sadness here, it kept ambushing you. Even reading a fucking letter, Tremaine thought bitterly.

He was glad that Becky had got his letter in time to send the foodstuffs he had requested: Red River cereal, oatmeal, dried fruit; but disappointed that she had sent them in such small quantities. Her little twist-tied bags bespoke a proximity to malls and supermarkets. Around them she had packed useless, sentimental things. Another mug, his desk lamp, two brass duck heads (he leaned back and shook his head at those), two framed pictures. The glass over the Monet print had cracked. Glass! Broken parts rattled in the clock radio.

The distance was working on her. In her last letter she had mentioned the possibility of visiting at Christmas. He was still working on a way to tell her that the reserve had no second-honeymoon potential that he could see, and much that would only make them feel their situation more keenly. Alone, you could get into a 'doing time' mentality, some long-haul myopia that helped.

Sophie and Rachel came by a little later to do their version of the tough cop/good cop routine. Obese, glowering Sophie working an unsubtle guilt angle – 'Oo, you're rich! Look at your new things! I wish I had some new things!' – which degenerated quickly into glum commands, delivered in a hopeless tone that did not anticipate compliance: 'Gimme some candy (the dried fruit). I like a little radio. You got glasses, I need a glass.' It was an old routine, which had not always failed; Sophie smiled sometimes, while not ceasing to frown. Rachel, her slim pretty sidekick, flirted meanwhile. 'Aren't you going to be nice and give me some snack. Just a teensy-weensy' – squirming her slender shoulders and hips, her dark slanted eyes sparkling – 'little tiny' – signing a minuscule portion with her thumb and forefinger – 'tiny snack.' She sucked her lower lip: 'I got no nice pictures on my walls.'

He offered them the broken clock radio if they wanted it. Rachel jammed it into her ski jacket pocket, the cord hanging out. 'Oh, thank you thank you thank you.' Immediately, he knew he had made a mistake. The fact that the radio was broken was of crucial importance to him; it might not be to others. After he had shut the door, it was yanked open again. 'Just a teensy weensy little green banana,' wheedled Rachel. Behind her, Sophie rubbed her stomach through her ski jacket.

'No,' he scowled. He shut the door and yanked the curtains, Roy's tongue-print now white.

No matter how cordially a begging session began, always it ended with a demand that in his view went over the top and left him feeling put upon, besieged. The students seemed almost to want the visits to end on a bad note. They came back to ensure it. Yet, unlike him, they did not hold grudges. 'Be careful what you give them. Especially when it comes to food,' the assistant superintendent had warned on his visit, late in August, to bring the new curriculum materials. 'You can create a monster in no time.' Tremaine, rebelling at what he perceived to be the spirit of the law, was finally trying to obey its letter. He *had* created a monster, or at least a persistent difficulty.

Sitting out of sight in the other room, he read the *Globe and Mail* Becky had sent. His interest flagged; it worked best if he treated it as a kind of test, closing his eyes and trying to recall the main points of each article. The air outside was purple-grey, the colour of a bruise. The thermometer still read minus 35. No – he looked closer: minus 36. It wasn't broken. The silence was broken by the whine of many snow machines, soft mosquito drones that seemed to come from all directions, and by the yip of Simon's dog, Weesaba. The name was Tremaine's stab at a spelling of Simon's clipped summons. Between these sounds was a deep silence, a thick soft cloth enveloping each one and keeping it isolated.

* * *

After lunch, he used the toilet and tried the tap again. Nothing. The bowl was full; it was either haul water to flush it or else start using Simon's outhouse. The janitor had removed the dirt and snow from a few metres of the water line and had piled evergreen boughs at intervals beside it. His game with Weesaba – holding a stick at shoulder height and urging the small furry dog to jump vainly at it – might have been his way of telling the new principal that the problem was serious. A strong and moody man, Simon had besides a predilection and gift for language that worked on many levels.

Reluctantly, Tremaine bundled up to go back to the Bay for a plastic water container. He bought two of the last three in stock, at $14.95 each. The water at the school was still on. He filled the twenty-litre drums and used a wheelbarrow to roll them back to the teacherage. He took one down to Sonder.

Sonder was appreciative, and a bit puzzled. 'I told Simon we need that water. We're not used to doing without it. Soft?' He grinned at Tremaine. 'He said he's ordered a heating coil, but until it gets here he thinks he can thaw it out and get it going.'

'Well, just in case.'

'Simon is a good man. I'd say we're lucky to have him.'

Tremaine agreed, though privately he did not think this was relevant.

'Guys like him are hard to come by now. Improvisers. Make do with what you've got. Did you see those spruce boughs?'

Tremaine, feeling that Simon's ability was not the question, though unable to voice a more material concern, nodded vaguely.

Sonder's boxes were stacked at the back of the kitchen, leaving a narrow channel into the living room. Sonder still looked gaunt, dark-eyed, though another day's length of whisker made him look more like a tired man growing a beard than the shipwreck survivor Tremaine had found standing amid his boxes in the back of Robert Wasnias's pickup. Some of his luggage was still missing; calls from the airport had failed to turn them up. '*Jomish*' – old man – '*jomish*,' the children, standing at the window, had begun to chant, and Sonder, misinterpreting, had smiled and waved. On the lunch break, looking bewildered, he asked Tremaine about Ada, his predecessor.

'Personal difficulties, I guess, would be the best way to put it,' Tremaine answered.

'You're loyal to her. That's good,' Sonder said. Tremaine had a sudden image of him as the green commander relieving a garrison in a war zone. 'Indian Affairs had no business sending a woman here. Teaching's one thing, but the principal's got to be in charge. That's no reflection on the people here. Maintaining discipline's the same set of problems anywhere, I'd say. I've taught in tougher schools than this. One look tells me that.' Sucking his lip, he allowed, 'But I guess they've got their staffing problems.'

Sonder took him beyond the boxes to show him some improvements he had made already. A slipcover his wife had sent with him was on the armchair and several calendar pictures were tacked up on the walls. He invited Tremaine back for a drink after dinner.

Tremaine felt uneasy talking in front of the living-room window with Sonder, even though it had nothing to do with the water problem. Simon was tinkering with his snow machine, close by. It seemed inconceivable that he could be working on metal parts without gloves in these temperatures. He told himself that he was being paranoid to be self-conscious about a white man's 'pow-wow'; probably condescending in some way, too. It snuck up on you, unpleasant knowledge about yourself. Perhaps active racism was in some sense a defence against such feelings.

As he was leaving, Sonder called him back. His brow was furrowed. 'Roy paid me a visit this afternoon. Roy ... what's-'s-name?'

'Roy Takenook?'

'That's it. He's a good-looking boy, isn't he?'

'Yes, he is.'

'Bit of a crazy laugh.'

'Yes.'

'He said you gave some girls a radio.'

'It was broken.'

'Oh.' Sonder sucked his lip. 'I see. Still, it might not have been a good idea.'

'I know. You're right.'

Tremaine was irritated by the mild rebuke, even though he sensed that part of the reason for it was Sonder's desire to take charge by dressing down the troops. His annoyance, however, was mixed with a dawning sense of security. Much as he liked her personally, things had slipped under Ada. She'd had a tough time. They all had.

That night, sipping Sonder's smuggled Scotch behind closed curtains, he experienced the same comfortable irritation – comfort *through* irritation – at seeing the new principal wind himself up into heartiness. It wasn't so much what he was doing as the fact that he saw fit, and was equipped, to do it. It was a sign of vital energy, a life sign. Monitoring himself, Tremaine found a more irregular pulse.

Sonder had taken the trouble to shave. He had also found CHLY; the radio on the coffee table was tuned to it. 'You mean to say,' he spoke from behind his glass, his eyes red-rimmed above the amber, 'that the little shack down the road, the one like a big privy with the smoke coming out, is their radio station?'

Tremaine, obscurely worried, nodded.

Sonder slapped his thigh with his free hand. 'I think that's fantastic! Out in the middle of nowhere but, by God, let's have a little music! Any one of these folks has more spunk than ten of the people we're working for. You and I, Don, we're the ones who're going to learn something.'

It wasn't so much disagreement that bothered Tremaine as much as a sense of irrelevance, as earlier with Sonder's praise of Simon as a mechanic. He smiled vaguely. Each time the 'program', after long periods of windy silence, resumed – usually with a teenage voice booming (too close to the mike) the time and the name of a tape: 'HELLO IT'S 9:13 AND THIS IS WHITE LION WHEN THE CHILDREN CRY' – Sonder cocked his head and listened, chuckling. Tremaine no longer played the station much. Propelled by a need to remain at least minimally plugged in to the local scene, he sometimes switched it on, usually catching the interval hiss, but it unnerved him.

Late in the evening, Sonder brought out a notepad and a box of curriculum materials and Tremaine opened the file folder he had brought.

Sonder said, 'I've been going over the attendance records since the start of term. A school can't function with this many students away each day.'

'It's hunting season.'

'It's never been good!' Sonder cried, then added in a softer voice, 'But you're right, it's worse lately.' His eyes were shining. 'Listen, Don. I've been reviewing all this' – he waved his hands over the boxed documents – 'and you know what I think?' Tremaine was eager to know. 'Balls to all of it! We could send the lot of it over to Simon's privy and not be any the worse off. It's not for these kids. I don't even think the people who wrote it up believe it is. They've got their mortgage payments. All right, I understand that. No grudges here. But let's you and I have an understanding right at the start. Whole language, or activity-based learning, or group dynamics – we'll tell them whatever they want to hear. But we'll concentrate on keeping order, try to fill a few more seats, and bring everyone up a notch in their reading and figures. What do you say? I need your honest opinion if we're going to work together.'

The relief that flooded Tremaine cancelled his ability to formulate, much less offer, an opinion. He merely raised his glass and muttered, 'Cheers!' willing at this moment to follow the new lieutenant anywhere.

Before he left, wishing to trade something for Sonder's confidence, he described the northern lights, which were peaking again. They had been beautiful when he arrived in August.

'Let's have a look!' Sonder said, inflamed. Drink in hand, he opened the back door; uneasily, Tremaine took his glass too. He looked around for Simon and saw the smoke from his stove.

It was the dark of the moon. The star-speckled blackness seemed to veer up, sheer, for miles, yet press close at the same time. Great bands of light, predominately pale green, but flushed in places with thrilling pinks, writhed like living things, organic curtains in a sensuous sway and wobble, from zenith to ground and across the visible sky.

'Splendid!' Sonder breathed.

They stayed outside as long as they could, long freezing seconds, while the savage cold nipped them from head to toe, playful bites that, cumulatively, inaugurated a numbness and a chill in the centre of oneself, behind the chest.

'Splendid!' Sonder said again, shutting the door, then

compromised the moment somewhat by adding, 'No wonder these people don't want to leave!'

But Tremaine was growing more tolerant of what he saw as the corollary of Sonder's enthusiasm, its tendency to overextend itself into vague effusions in which subtlety, or even common sense, was momentarily suspended.

Sunday morning was his time to stay in bed late. Relaxing, he told himself, even if he couldn't sleep. He read the book reviews in the *Globe* and copied down some titles to look for when he went to Thunder Bay for the winter meeting. The teacherage was warm, almost stuffy. Lying in bed, he imagined one of those winter scenes in a crystal ball, but with inside and outside reversed. Inside the tiny glass space was a furnished scene, with a miniature man under blankets; outside was a vast cold medium, an enveloping fluid with a layer of settled white flakes. His stomach prickled uncomfortably when he tried to extend the fantasy to a pair of giant hands picking up the paperweight, horizon-filling features blurring as something peered in, then shook the world to send the flakes swirling – the upset to his sense of scale made him feel dizzy, as though he were falling sideways.

Many families went to the Roman Catholic church behind the cemetery. A familiar hush hovered over the reserve, a poise or suspension that took Tremaine back to his childhood. Then, the whole day had seemed a waiting-for-something, a delicious expectancy, but when the something had never arrived, the expectancy had soured. Gradually the day had died for him, its drained blood replaced by a sweet jittery anxiety that could not nourish or sustain.

Becky's reasons for staying (which, since he had a contract to honour, amounted to leaving), seemed, when she tried to explain them, to allude to a similar process. 'Something kept on the back burner too long' – thickening, sticking, blackening; Tremaine extended the image for himself. Then she cried and said that wasn't it. But it was, he thought.

In the afternoon he went for his usual walk around the village. Despite the severe cold, he pushed himself to continue the habit. Apart from his morning push-ups it was his only exercise; and it was a minor, but faultless, way of joining the village life. He bundled himself up: long johns, shirt and pants, double socks, heavy wool sweater, scarf, then hooded parka and mitts and boots. Inside it all, he moved stiffly, with a cramped feeling that was somehow akin to power. When the big dogs rushed him, with dirty bellies and matted yellow-white fur, he raised his arm in alarm and saw a log-like green shape float up in an almost formal salute. Though he had no stick, it was enough. Tails dragging between their smeared hams, they slunk off.

He walked in the middle of the road so he could be seen by the snowmobilers. Their racket made it seem he was walking in city traffic. Engines and drivers screamed to and fro past him, bumping on the hard rutted roadway, clumping on gappy boardwalks, crashing into bush and clawing their way back up over branches onto the road. The lake ice was not yet safe in all places. This was the month, this and April, when radios were turned on fearfully each morning. Seldom did a season start, or end, without several people and their machines going through the ice.

They love the winter, they can get around, get out – the superintendent had enthused at his interview. And Tremaine had begun to relax, realizing that there were no wrong answers.

The boardwalk up the south side of the peninsula was in the lee of the short stands of spruce and tamarack, but it always felt coldest, because of the unbroken expanse of the lake it gave onto. Most of the houses were along this stretch. Frozen laundry swayed on clotheslines. Smoke issued from the stovepipes. Ravens walked about the yards and incinerators, hopping up to perches with croaking cr-r-uck sounds that made the caw of the southern crow seem musical. Snow machines clattered along the pebbly ice near the shore. A little farther out were the ice holes, some black with water, others grey-skinned. Sophie's great-grandmother, Dorothy, who had sold him the slippers and bead doilies, stood by a pail, her colourful dress flapping in the wind, while one of her many grandsons poked with a long-handled chisel. She waved, as she never failed to do, and Tremaine waved back. Near the end of the boardwalk, just past Rachel's house, was a blackened square where a house had burnt down, now strewn with garbage and two hopping, proprietorial ravens, each working his side. As he passed, Tremaine looked among the charred wreckage for the clock radio but did not see it.

Hurrying home, he felt the cold seeping into his legs, stiffening his gait. Several times, he yanked off his deerhide mittens to press his hands to his forehead and cheeks, for the brief relief this brought. Almost home, he met Sonder, coming up the boardwalk with a paper bag. It was painful to talk to him with the door so close.

Sonder opened the bag to show him the slippers he had bought. 'I guess you've got a pair of these.'

Tremaine smiled with stiff cheeks. 'Most of my Christmas shopping was done by September.'

Sonder scowled. 'I like initiative. But I'm not going to turn myself into somebody's cottage industry.' His expression softened; it was not inappropriate that the junior teacher be exposed as the easier mark.

Warming up inside, sighing with the profound pleasure of rubbing his hands together in a heated room, Tremaine wondered about Sonder's scowl. He didn't think the older man was aware of doing it. Seasoned teachers developed such tics, one of the hazards of making faces in front of an audience whose reactions to them were constrained. You exaggerated yourself, without meaning to.

It was dark now. He opened a can of sardines and had them on bread, to avoid dirtying another dish. He thought he was reading Sonder right in not going down for a visit tonight. One of the goals, too ingrained to be written down on the notepad, would be to maintain a balance of personal and professional relations.

He finished the *Globe*, then heated some water and had a bird bath. He did the dishes in his bathwater and rinsed them with another hot kettle. He masturbated to get to sleep.

Monday, the cold was unbroken. Minus 39. After a breakfast of green banana and Wonder bread with jam, Tremaine tried the water. Surprisingly, after a few burps of gas, it came on. He let the brown meltwater through, then left it on a trickle. He was mildly confused, though grateful; he hadn't heard or seen Simon at work. But when he tried to flush the toilet, he watched in horror as the water rose slowly to the top of the bowl and over, depositing the contents on the floor in a spreading pool. Tears of frustration blinded him. Working frantically, he was still a half hour cleaning it up.

The Wasnias and Wasoon children were huddled, shivering, on the front step. When they saw him, they pleaded to be allowed to wait inside. 'Is cold, Don ... so cold.' Hands tugged at his coat. 'Look' – a skeleton clacking of white teeth – 'see me shiver.'

'You know the rules,' Tremaine said, but his face must have said: We'll see. Pushed from behind, he worked the sticking lock and squeezed through ridiculously, afraid to offer them an opening.

At the staff meeting, he took it up with Sonder. Sonder had his Robinson Crusoe face back, eyes wide in stubble. He asked Susannah Sweetfoot, the classroom assistant, what was usually done in the winter.

Susannah merely smiled and murmured, 'The children get so cold,' as though it were a uniquely redeeming quality.

'I suppose we could let them into the hall by the coat racks,' Sonder mused, looking from Tremaine to Susannah. 'But not into the classroom. School starts at nine o'clock.'

Tremaine nodded, thinking that Simon, from his room opposite the hall, could keep them there, just as Weesaba backed down any creature that went too near Simon's tent. He stood behind Sonder as he opened the door and pointed to the benches underneath the coat racks. Silent, the dark faces looked up at him as he explained the rules. Ada had got this far, but only on the first day.

From the small east window in his classroom, Tremaine watched the sun clear the far low trees, a pale globe creeping through a severe band of pink into a softer blue tinged with orange. Eight forty-five. Daylight came and went with the school day, now. When he turned from the window, he saw that several children had stolen in on stockinged feet and were sitting quietly in their desks. Damn! Across the hall, Sonder was leading several of the smaller children around his room.

'Was getting too crowded, Don, man,' whined Jeremy Wasoon.

'Only in your seats,' Tremaine commanded, knowing he was placing rules just ahead of their advance. 'Nothing from the shelves.' The rule was arbitrary; but so were they all, finally.

Turning back to the window he saw a bent figure with what

looked like an armful of sticks advancing out on the ice of the lake. Sticks planted upright in a meandering path behind the figure described the course he had taken. He narrowed his eyes in interest. The scene seemed somehow archetypal – the bent slow progress into the rising winter sun with an armload of sticks – but he could not decide its meaning. Ahead of the figure, he saw with growing fear, were patches of grey ice, even, perhaps, open water.

'Sit down, Bartholomew,' he said to a boy who had crept up to peer over the sill. When he saw that he was ignored, he blamed it on Bartholomew's interest in the distant figure, and asked, 'Who is it?'

'*Jomish*. Old man.'

'Which jomish?'

'Gabriel.' Bartholomew crossed his eyes and covered his teeth with his lips. There seemed no mockery, only accurate observation in his portrayal of a cross-eyed, toothless old man Tremaine had seen sitting on the steps at the Bay store.

'What's he doing?'

'He check the ice.' And Tremaine understood that the weaving path the old man marked with his lines of sticks would allow the first traffic across the frozen lake.

Watching Gabriel plant his sticks, he saw the progress of winter laid out before him. The sticks would cross Bitter Lake, remain there through six months of snow and freezing gales, and then, in a return rite, be collected again, just before break-up. He didn't see how he could stand it. Any strength he had built up seemed to fall from him like a casing, exposing a new soft creature, helpless in the cold.

'Sit down, Bartholomew,' he said, remembering. When he turned he saw all of the children in the room, most of them now, standing on their desks to see out the window. 'Sit down, all of you!' he barked, hearing his shrillness.

Sonder came into the room. He fixed the students with a glare that made their return to their seats, their hands folded, his work. He warned Tremaine to expect a fire alarm just after nine o'clock. No need to evacuate the building; he just wanted Simon to test the bell.

Sonder kept his eye on the slowly advancing figure while he spoke, rubbing his whiskered cheeks; but he did not ask. Tremaine felt the man's thought processes as if they were his own. Too much curiosity, an avowal of newness, might undermine his authority. Ada, always pleasant and inquiring, had been too blatant in her desire to master the new locale.

After the Lord's Prayer, chanted in English and then mumbled in Ojibway, the fire bell rang.

Tremaine headed off the quickest at the door, herding them back to their seats. The boys were grinning, the smallest looking to the largest for confirmation. The girls clapped hands over their ears, mouths O-ing in pain. He checked their eyes: sparkling, trading glances. An adventure in confusion, in discord. Only two were really crying. Linda's head was down, her shoulders shaking; but when he touched her back she straightened up and began brushing at the tears bouncing off her cheeks.

Mary Ellen, however, was in trouble. Her hands were balled in tiny fists jammed at her reddened ears. She jerked her head from side to side, then up at Tremaine, tears leaking from her eyes, her mouth spasmodic with moans that were audible in the minute pauses between the clanging notes.

Remembering, then, her many earaches, which could be otitis media, he became afraid. Waving at the others to remain where they were, he bundled her out of the classroom. She leaned one fist-covered ear into his side; he could feel her sobs through the hand on her shoulder.

He left her for a moment by the coat room and went into Simon's room. The janitor was fussing at the fire alarm box, Sonder behind him. They couldn't make the sound stop. It whirred and jangled and clanged and roared, a clamour like a thickened medium in which it was difficult to move, hard even to think. Tremaine could think of nothing to suggest, no question to shout. He had no idea how they worked.

Mary Ellen was standing where he had left her, bawling. He thought she might actually be screaming, her face was so contorted. He was almost glad for the concealing noise. Could he take her outside? It was forty below. Perhaps he could bundle her into her coat, or into his, which could be folded over like a blanket. But what would the piercing air, and the still shrill bell, do to her damaged ears; how long would they wait, out there?

The sound stopped. It withdrew like a presence, leaving empty space. In that space, Mary Ellen was sobbing, gulping for air as she said brokenly, over and over, 'My ears … my ears … my ears.'

The ringing began again.

Tremaine looked over his shoulder with rage, as if to find a demon he could throw himself at. The kids in Sonder's room were running around, making a wild game of it. Over the wild clamour, he heard raised voices, then a growled, 'Fuck it then!' Then a slammed door. As if it were his own, he felt Simon's humiliation in the face of the broken mechanism. Sonder, with a white, stricken face, brushed by him and slammed the door to his room. No one must witness his attempts to quiet the children, or himself.

Mary Ellen was stamping her feet up and down in pain, swaying from side to side. Tremaine felt himself about to explode with helplessness. He was afraid to leave her to trip the circuit breaker. Or did it run on batteries? Surely Simon would return. These instants felt like minutes, but they couldn't be. Simon would return.

He got down on his knees, at eye level with Mary Ellen, gripping her shoulders. Through the brimming slits between her eyelids he saw pain and fright wound up to a breaking point. He held her to him and then pushed her back slightly – pain this deep could not be hugged away. Dimly he was aware of the door to his room opening, faces clustering nearby.

He pressed his hands around Mary Ellen's, and then, by a pressure on her fists, urged her to drop her hands so that his own, larger, could cover her ears better. The only thing now was to seal her off, block the sound. Her hands gave way at the pressure from his, and he rushed to cover her ears, cupping his hands. In the instant nothing was against her ears, she screamed, a howl so piercing it was clearly audible.

Pinned to her to protect her, he could do nothing further. The moment – her agony and his futile shouted comfort, frozen in an aspic of utter chaos – was worse even than any he had imagined in the days after his arrival, before he had stopped imagining. He was armless now. He felt her fumbling at her pockets for something, he supposed a Kleenex. He had some but he was armless.

As the terrible din abruptly ceased, she offered him something, held it up to him with one trembling hand, while her eyes sent a new ray of appeal, or atonement, through her tears. Unable to take his hands from her ears, he saw, between his arms, a blue Bic pen which for a few moments completely baffled him.

Acknowledgements

Thanks to the editors of the following magazines, in which many of these stories first appeared: *The New Quarterly, The Fiddlehead, The Malahat Review, Descant, Dandelion,* and *Blood & Aphorisms.* Thanks also to the Ontario Arts Council, for financial support.

HEATHER BARNES

Mike Barnes is the author of *Calm Jazz Sea* (Brick Books), a collection of poems which was shortlisted for the Gerald Lampert Memorial Award in 1996. His short stories have appeared in many magazines, including *The New Quarterly*, *The Fiddlehead*, *The Malahat Review*, *Descant*, *Dandelion*, and *Blood & Aphorisms*. Some of his stories are forthcoming in both *99: Best Canadian Stories* and *The Journey Prize Anthology*. He lives in Toronto.